For the first time in her life, she was tempted, very, very tempted, to swallow her shyness and take a chance.

To break out of the shell that had gotten her nowhere in life. Flirt a little. Walk on the wild side.

Well, at least cross the sidewalk. Actually *walking* on the wild side might be more then she could handle.

All her life she'd been known as the good girl: dependable, smart, obedient. Conventional Katie. It used to be a plus.

Curiosity over the sexy stranger, helped along by the anonymity of a fruit costume, overrode Katie's natural tendency to be reserved.

Walk on the wild side, Katie. Just a step or two.

Dear Reader,

Now that the holidays are over, I'll bet you need some serious R and R, and what better way to escape the everyday and recharge your spirit than with Silhouette Romance? We'll take you on the rewarding, romantic journey from courtship to commitment!

This month you're in for some very special surprises! First, beloved Carolyn Zane returns with *The Cinderella Inheritance* (#1636), a tender, rollicking, triumphant rags-to-riches love story. Then Karen Rose Smith brings you the next installment in the amazing SOULMATES series. In *With One Touch* (#1638), Brooke Pennington can magically heal animals, but only Dr. Nate Stanton has the power to cure her own aching heart.

If the greatest lesson in life is love, then you won't want to miss these two Romance novels. In Susan Meier's *Baby on Board* (#1639), the first in her DAYCARE DADS miniseries, Caro Evans is hired to teach dark, guarded Max Riley how to care for his infant daughter—and how to love again. And in *The Prince's Tutor* (#1640) by Nicole Burnham, Amanda Hutton is used to instructing royal *children* about palace protocol, but not a full-grown playboy prince with other lessons in mind....

Appearances can be deceiving, especially in Cathie Linz's *Sleeping Beauty & the Marine* (#1637), about journalist Cassandra Jones who loses the glasses and colors her hair to find out if gentlemen prefer blondes, and hopes a certain marine captain doesn't! Then former bad-boy Matt Webster nearly goes bananas when he agrees to be the pretend fiancé of one irresistible virgin, in Shirley Jump's *The Virgin's Proposal* (#1641).

Next month, look for popular Romance author Carla Cassidy's 50th book, part of a duo called THE PREGNANCY TEST, about two women with two very different test results!

Happy reading!

Mary-Theresa Hussey

Mary-Theresa Hussey
Senior Editor

Please address questions and book requests to:
Silhouette Reader Service
U.S.: 3010 Walden Ave., P.O. Box 1325, Buffalo, NY 14269
Canadian: P.O. Box 609, Fort Erie, Ont. L2A 5X3

The Virgin's Proposal

SHIRLEY JUMP

SILHOUETTE *Romance*®
Published by Silhouette Books
America's Publisher of Contemporary Romance

First, to Janet Dean, whose wisdom and many critiques
helped shape this book into what it is today—
I wouldn't be here without her unflagging support. To
Suzanne Simmons, Tina St. John and Suzanne Brockmann,
for encouraging me over the years.
And finally, to my husband, Jeff, the real hero in my life.

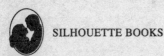 SILHOUETTE BOOKS

ISBN 0-373-19641-5

THE VIRGIN'S PROPOSAL

Copyright © 2003 by Shirley Kawa-Jump

Visit Silhouette at www.eHarlequin.com

Printed in U.S.A.

SHIRLEY JUMP

has been a writer ever since she learned to read. She sold her first article at the age of eleven and from there, became a reporter and finally a freelance writer. However, she always maintained the dream of writing fiction, too. Since then, she has made a full-time career out of writing, dividing her time between articles, non-fiction books and romance. With a husband, two children and a houseful of pets, inspiration abounds in her life, giving her good fodder for writing and a daily workout for her sense of humor.

Dear Reader,

Six years ago, I began a story about a woman in a banana suit on a street corner and a guy on a motorcycle, but I didn't know who they were or why they were there. After seven pages, I put the story aside, my moment of inspiration over.

A few years later, I stumbled across those pages and laughed all over again, realizing I had a great start to a book. I sketched out who Matt and Katie might be, then began to write. Their story is my favorite out of all the manuscripts I've written and it's a special thrill to see it become my first published romance novel.

Shirley Jump

Chapter One

Standing on a street corner in a banana suit was not the most humiliating thing to happen in Katie's life, but it came in at a close second.

Dressed from head to toe in yellow felt, she barely remembered what the word *dignity* meant. She'd checked hers the minute Sarah had talked her into masquerading as a piece of fruit, all to increase sales.

"Hey Chiquita! Can you peel for me?" A carload of teenagers screamed past her. She might as well have been the Soak-the-Bloke clown for all the respect she'd received. Apparently, a five-foot-three, twenty-four-year-old woman in a banana suit was the funniest thing in the tiny town of Mercy, Indiana, today. What kind of suicidal tendencies had made her mention the idea of doing something unique to boost sales to Sarah, soon-to-be-ex-best friend and business partner?

The store. It was all she thought about. Sales had been low when they'd opened a year ago and kept dropping. The rent was due in two weeks, and unfortunately, their bank account didn't have a big enough balance to cover it. Katie and Sarah had yet to find a way to crack the hold their competition, Flowers and More, a shop in the nearby city of Lawford, had on Mercy. Plenty of weddings, bar mitzvahs, showers and funerals happened around here, but hardly anyone was buying from A Pair of Posies.

If there was some way to get people to notice the store, maybe Katie wouldn't feel like such a failure—both personally and business-wise. She was desperate to make a go of the store—desperate enough to wear the fruit suit.

She sighed. The four-tone Ford with the teens came swerving back around the corner. "You'd be King Kong's dream!"

She ignored them, her cheeks hot. Sales or no sales, the costume was humiliating. Thank God the foam head covered most of her face. The last thing she wanted was anyone finding out it was *her* under the peel.

She straightened the sign advertising their sale on fruit baskets, then noticed a motorcycle, gleaming in chrome and black, roar down the street toward her and slip into one of the front spaces. She bit her lip and steeled herself for another onslaught of pubescent humor. The rider pulled off his helmet and swung a denim-clad leg over the bike.

Oh. My. God. The man was no teenager and no joke. Motorcycle Man had extra-dark Hershey-brown hair that raked across his brows and set off eyes the color of a twilight sky. He was tall, taller than she and her banana head put together, and lean in a way that said he hadn't spent hours on a couch playing potato. Stonewashed jeans molded his hips; a white T-shirt hugged his chest. Topped with a battered chestnut-brown leather jacket, he looked as if he'd stepped out of a James Dean movie.

And yet, he looked familiar. But try as she might, she couldn't quite place a name with his face.

He glanced at her as he passed, smiling at her costume. A shiver tingled down her spine. With his slow, easy grin and confident step, he looked like the kind of man who knew exactly what the word *pleasure* meant and how to give it as well as he got it. *That* was a skimpy area on Katie's personal résumé.

"Great marketing idea," he said before disappearing into the shop.

Katie straightened her tilting foam head and wished men with movie-star looks would only stop in on days when she didn't look ready for trick-or-treating.

Just once, I wonder what it would be like to be with a man like that.

For the first time in her life, she was tempted, very, very tempted, to swallow her shyness and take a chance. To break out of the shell that had gotten her nowhere in life. Talk to him. Flirt a little. Walk on the wild side.

Well, at least cross the sidewalk. Actually *walking* on the wild side might be more than she could handle. And, according to the breakup letter from her ex-fiancé, Steve Spencer, it was something she would never do. When she'd proved to be too boring for his tastes, Steve had left her at the altar and run off with Katie's bridesmaid—a woman who gave him exactly what he wanted, when he wanted it. Because of that, Katie had become the most pitied person in town. All her life she'd been the good girl: dependable, obedient. It used to be a plus. But all it had done was make her a grown-up doormat.

Not to mention, still a virgin at twenty-four. She used to be proud she'd stuck to her guns, held out for her wedding night. Now she felt like the world's biggest idiot.

Make that the world's biggest banana, she amended.

For a few seconds, she stopped thinking about the shop and the horrible day she'd had so far. Her mind turned to

Motorcycle Man and how a glimpse of him had her thinking about tossing her morals right out the window. They hadn't gotten her very far anyway—just alone and dressed like one of the four food groups.

My hormones have launched a mental coup, she thought. There was no other explanation for the fact she was still reeling from his smile. *Imagine what a kiss from him would be like,* her conspiratorial mind whispered.

Who was he? He certainly didn't live here in town, though maybe he used to and that's why he looked familiar. A man like him, a man who would leave broken hearts in his path as surely as the Presbyterian church clock would chime the hour ten minutes late, couldn't buy a soda at the Bowl-a-Rama without spurring excited twitters among the female half of Mercy's population of 4,036.

Kate wiped away the sweat beading along her brow. The late-April sun beat down, roasting her like the turkeys in a bag her mother cooked every Thanksgiving. She was tempted to toss the banana suit and rejoin the human race. She could grab an icy soda out of the fridge and plant herself under the air conditioner until icicles hung from her nose.

Katie ducked her head, moving back into the cool shade of the awning. And collided with something tall and solid. She teetered, then began to topple over, heavy banana head first. Strong arms righted her before she hit the concrete. ''Thanks.'' She pivoted in suit-restricted geisha-girl steps to see the identity of her rescuer.

Could her day get any more humiliating? Motorcycle Man was standing behind her, a bundle of roses cushioned in one arm and that same easy grin lighting up his face. ''Are you okay?''

''Yeah,'' she managed. ''Thanks for catching me before I became a banana split.''

He smiled. "It's not every day I get a chance to rescue a banana in distress."

Curiosity, helped along by the anonymity of a fruit costume, overrode Katie's natural tendency to be reserved. *Walk on the wild side, Katie. Just a step or two. Besides, he's a customer—no harm in being friendly.*

"It must be the most a*peel*ing part of your day." The dry humor slipped from her tongue as if she talked this way every day. *Geez, put a costume on me and I become Jay Leno.* "Or maybe it's better than slipping on one...."

He laughed and put up a hand. "Truce. I guess you've heard your share of jokes this morning."

"Yours just added to the total. I'm at lucky thirteen now."

"Sorry."

She flashed him a smile which she knew he couldn't see. "Now that you've teased and nearly toppled me, the least you can do is tell me who you are."

He extended his hand. "Matt Webster."

The name immediately clicked. Handsome and rich renegade son of the Webster family. A few years older than her, so not someone Katie had really known. She did remember the huge wedding-of-the-century his family had held for him ten years or so ago, but then he'd left town and no one had heard much about him since.

She pulled off her glove and shook. His hand was slightly rough and callused, but large, capable and strong. And bare of a wedding ring, she noted. "Katie Dole."

She saw him try to hold back the laughter, but it burst out all the same. "You're joking, right?"

"I wish."

"No relation to the fruit company, I presume?"

She shook her head, the foam head bobbing. "I'm not that lucky."

"Are you related to Jack Dole?"

She nodded. "He's my oldest brother. Then there's Luke, Mark and Nate. There are a lot of bananas in the Dole family tree."

He laughed. "Well, Miss Dole, it was a *delicious* pleasure to meet you."

His hand slipped out of hers and with it went a warmth that had nothing to do with the hot day. She scrambled for a witty reply…nothing. Dressed as a piece of fruit, she felt a tad out of her element as a woman. Short of tucking herself into a massive bowl of ice cream and drizzling chocolate sauce down her torso, she didn't think her banana costume made her look very appealing to a man like him.

So she stood there like the village idiot as he waved and got back on the motorcycle, tucking the flowers into the compartment behind him before roaring away.

That man was definitely dangerous, always had been, if his reputation was any indication. The kind of guy who was out of her league, sexually, physically…every way. A man who lived on the brink. Katie had never lived anywhere close to the edge. She was too afraid of hurtling over it and into a canyon of heartache.

As if he had some kind of death wish, Matt pushed his Harley to the limit. The town where he'd spent what some would call his formative years rushed by in a blur of impressions: the Langdon Street sign that still bent to the right, eleven years after his convertible had given it a new shape; Amos Wintergreen's farm, where Matt and his friends had tipped cows until Amos's Labrador drove them off his land; the county jail, where he'd spent many a night paying for what his father called "bad choices."

The wind whipped at his jacket, pushing him to turn

around and go back to Pennsylvania. He had a business there, a life. He didn't need to be in Mercy, he told himself.

With a determined twist, Matt revved the engine of the 1974 Sportster and the sleek machine beneath him lunged forward.

The image of the woman in the banana suit popped into his head. The memory erased the growing tension in his neck. He chuckled. She must be mighty brave to put on such a public display in a small town, especially *this* small town.

His imagination was drifting toward what she'd look like beneath the peel when the bike shuddered and the engine began to cough and stall. Matt squeezed the handlebar brakes and brought the motorcycle to a grinding, definitely-bad-for-the-engine halt.

"Damn!" he swore at the defiant mass of steaming metal. The head gasket had blown and was spewing oil everywhere. Slick, dark liquid sprayed over his boots, across his T-shirt, trickled down the sleeves of his leather jacket. He set the bike on its kickstand, grabbed a rag from the toolbox strapped to the back and rubbed off the worst of it.

He was still two miles away from what used to be home. How ironic. Instead of the triumphant return he'd envisioned, he'd have to limp back to his parents' house, hauling a several-hundred-pound pile of metal to boot. He swore twice more, cursing the fates resoundingly. But they didn't listen. They'd given up on him long ago.

He began pushing it along the side of the road. The sun beat down, cooking him inside his leather jacket. He glanced at the cooler strapped to the back. A waste of time. The container had been empty of anything carbonated for the last ten miles. What he wouldn't do for an ice-cold beer, or two or ten, right about now.

It had been eleven years since he'd dropped to the bottom

and picked himself up, but some days—especially this day—the siren call of alcohol was loud and insistent.

For the thousandth time, Matt wondered why he'd thought it would be a good idea to come back.

At the end of the day, Katie headed into the air-conditioned shop, grateful she and Sarah had scraped together enough money to repair the aging cooling system. She peeled off the suit, stripping down to her shorts and tank.

"We had three orders for fruit baskets, so our idea boosted business. Not enough, though." Sarah seated herself on a stool, popping open a can of soda and handing it to Katie, who promptly guzzled down half. "Was it as much fun as it looked?"

"Oh, so much more fun. I can't believe you talked me into doing that." Katie slipped off the yellow felt coverings on her sneakers. "You should try it sometime."

"I'd be glad to. But the suit won't fit for a couple months!" She patted her stomach, the mountainous bulge announcing her pregnancy, now in its ninth month.

It had been three years since Jack, Katie's oldest brother, had married Sarah. Ever since, Katie had been awaiting the day a tiny voice called her Auntie Katie. Her brother Luke's daughter was eleven and living in California, too far away to spoil. It wasn't a family of her own, but it was the next best thing. Buying bibs and stuffed animals also kept her from thinking too hard about her own life—not that there'd been much of one to think about. She'd been stuck in glue for the past year, not moving forward with anything other than the store. Work was the only thing that filled the emptiness that crept around her when she flipped the sign to Closed.

It also helped her avoid the one thing she feared. Failure.

Katie had yet to be a success at anything. She'd had good grades in high school, but not good enough to get a college scholarship. She'd joined the debate team and publicly frozen at her first competition. She'd dated the captain of the football team, but had been dumped at the altar. And now, the store—her dream—was close to financial ruin. Another imminent failure, if she didn't take some action.

Katie propped open the door and dragged in the sign. "I'm glad to hear we had a few sales. We needed them."

"I know. The road construction isn't helping. The rent—" Sarah stopped when the door jangled.

Katie immediately recognized the woman who entered the store. Olivia Maguire, owner of the only interior design business in the Mercy area. Tall, thin and dressed in silvery-blue, she sailed into the room, straight for the counter. "Is that your design in the window?" she asked Sarah, pointing to an exotic silk display.

"Yes, it is." Sarah said.

"Good. I'll take two of those. As fast as you can get them to me." She paced the store, her movements quick, exact. "And one of these," she pointed to an elaborate vase filled with antique silk roses. "And three of those." She gestured to a design Sarah had put out yesterday, a retro planter with bright flowers. "How soon can I have them?"

"We'd be happy to create those for you." Katie proffered her hand when Sarah remained mute, mouth agape. "I'm Katie Dole, one of the owners. This is Sarah—"

"Yes, I know. I believe we've met once before, at a charity function or something." She waved her hand vaguely. "Besides, it's a small town. Everyone knows everyone *and* their business." Olivia gave Katie's hand a short, firm shake. "I'm Olivia Maguire. I own Renew Interior Designs. Right now, I have three clients who need arrangements. I drove by, saw that interesting one in the window and decided to stop." She spun on her heel, taking in the shop. "I like what I see. I normally use the Lawford shop, but I'd like to give yours a try, if you have time in your schedule."

"Certainly." Katie shot a glance at Sarah. "We could probably have those arrangements to you in three days." Sarah turned, grabbed the order pad and started writing.

"Make it two and you have a deal." Olivia laid some money on the counter for a down payment.

Sarah nodded, her gaze on the cash. "Okay."

"Wonderful." Olivia handed Katie a foil-embossed business card. "Call me when they're ready." Then she left.

When the door shut, Katie let out a breath. "This is great! It's the break we've been waiting for!"

Sarah took the card, turning it over and over in her hand. "That could be a *great* account for us. It would get our name in front of people with money to spend, the same people who buy loads of flowers for their houses and churches. People like the Callahans and the Simpsons and the Websters..." Sarah's jaw dropped. "That's right! Olivia's our direct ticket to them."

"What do you mean?"

"Don't you remember? Olivia Maguire used to be married to their son..." She waved her hand, searching for the name. "Matt! That's it. The one who was always in trouble. Maybe you don't remember him. He was a few years ahead of us in school and I barely remember what he looked like myself."

"Funny you should mention him." Katie took another sip of her pop. "The man who was here earlier—"

"The incredibly gorgeous one?"

Katie laughed. "You noticed?"

"I'm pregnant, not blind," Sarah replied. "What about him?"

"He said he was Matt Webster."

"*The* Matt Webster?" Sarah picked up the card again. "*Olivia's* Matt?" She rubbed her belly absently. "Didn't they break up after they lost their baby? The family kept everything hush-hush. It's been what, ten years, since then?"

"I don't know. We didn't exactly have an in-depth conversation under the awning." Katie smiled. "All I saw was, well, his eyes," she admitted.

"Did you ask him out?"

"Sarah, I was wearing a banana suit."

"So? Doesn't mean you can't be spontaneous." She wagged a finger at Katie. "Try a little spontaneity, you might like it."

"Spoken by the queen of spontaneity herself. Heck, you even got married on the spur of the moment."

"Eloping is exciting and romantic," Sarah said with a flourish of her hand. "I like to live for the moment, rather than let it pass me by."

Katie considered Sarah's words as she worked on the roses in the cooler. She changed the water and added floral preservative before placing the flowers back into the containers. The banana suit, while embarrassing, had also emboldened her and given her the chutzpah to exchange witty repartee with a sexy stranger. It had been a new feeling, a liberating one. In her twenty-four years, she hadn't taken many chances and the ones she had—Steve, the store— hadn't exactly been successful. Maybe if she changed her approach, the outcome would be different.

For too many years, she'd been Conventional Katie, always predictable, never stepping out of bounds, even when the ball was hurtling toward her head. That kind of reliability had led her to a broken heart and a year of lonely evenings.

"I've been thinking," Katie said. "You know what today is, don't you?"

"Uh huh," Sarah replied with a sympathetic look. "I didn't want to mention it, though. Figured it might make it hard for you to be a jolly banana."

Katie laughed. Sarah had always been able to erase Katie's blue moods. Lord knew there'd been plenty of those in the last year. "It would have been my first anniversary, *if* Steve hadn't left me at the altar."

"In the end, a very good thing."

"I didn't think so at the time, but I do now. If I'd married him and then he'd taken off with someone else, it would have been worse." Katie plucked a pale peach rose from the bucket and sniffed the delicate fragrance. Sarah's motto sounded like the perfect antidote for Katie's stagnant life. *Live for the moment, before it passes you by. And leaves you old and alone,* she amended. "I've been moping long enough. It's time for a change."

"Good for you!" Sarah settled back on the stool. "What kind of change are you thinking about?"

"First, I'm going to overindulge in chocolate," Katie said. "And then, well…" She thought of Matt Webster and how a smile from him had set off fireworks in her belly. "I *might* just go for something a little more decadent."

Fate sure had a twisted sense of humor. There wasn't a single Hershey Bar or Sara Lee double chocolate layer cake in the seven-aisle store that passed for a supermarket in Mercy. Katie supposed it was a mark of small-town charm, but for a girl craving chocolate and calories, it left a lot to be desired. Being mid-week, the shelves and freezer case were already empty of anything remotely indulgent. Muttering in defeat, Katie grabbed a box of fruit-flavored Popsicles and laid it in the row of groceries in her basket, arranged in order of her coupons.

She wandered up and down the aisles, in no hurry to return to her empty apartment. As she rounded a display of spaghetti sauce, she heard a familiar voice. Then another. She stopped in her tracks and peeked beyond the jars.

"Oh, Stevie, get the extra cheese popcorn," purred a woman draped on Katie's ex-fiancé's arm. The feline vixen in a lavender dress was none other than Barbara—ex-bridesmaid and traitor.

In tenth grade, Barbara and Katie had met in a study group that managed to ace Miss Marchand's biology class. They'd become friends and stayed in touch during college. When Barbara returned from four years in Boston and had trouble finding a job, she'd seemed depressed. So Katie often invited her along to join her and Steve as a threesome, or with a friend of Steve's, thinking it would be the boost Barbara needed. Too trusting by far, Katie later realized she'd been the conduit to a secret affair instead.

Why hadn't she put the pieces together when Barbara caught a sudden case of the flu the morning of the wedding? While Katie was standing in front of a hundred people waiting for a groom who never came, Barbara had been off consummating a different union.

On *Katie's* honeymoon. With *Katie's* groom.

And Steve—he'd probably been drinking *their* champagne in the crystal glasses *her* mother had bought, toasting *another* woman in a negligee. An eager woman. One who wouldn't make him wait until the vows were said and done. And he'd probably been finding the exact kind of excitement he'd told Katie she lacked.

She'd heard they'd moved to Lansing, Michigan. But clearly, they were back, and sharing their love—based on a mutual admiration for wrestling and Coors beer—with all of Mercy. *Ugh.*

A year's worth of anger, which Conventional Katie had kept under a tight, polite lid, boiled up inside her. She'd vowed to go on with her life, but that didn't mean she'd forgotten. They'd betrayed her, even going so far as to keep the shower gifts, and she'd taken it all without a word, while Barbara sipped from Katie's Waterford and kissed Katie's groom.

She wondered if she could be arrested for assaulting them with an extra-large box of Orville Redenbacher's.

"Excuse me, miss."

Katie wheeled around. Standing directly behind her, with a shopping cart full of the gastrointestinal nightmares that only bachelors seemed to buy, was Matt Webster.

She was now in her own clothes, no banana suit to hide behind. It was a perfect chance to test the waters of her new spontaneity resolution, right in front of Barbara and Steve. Take a chance. Dip a toe in the wild side.

A second peek around the corner and she saw Steve, one hand on Barbara's waist, strolling down the aisle, debating popcorn choices. They were going to see her in a minute— the lovey-dovey couple encountering the lonely, jilted bride. She imagined the pity on their faces, the knowing smiles that said she was the unfortunate one, the one who hadn't gone on, a year after the fiasco.

It was high time she gave everyone in town something better to talk about. She was tired of being boring, dependable Katie. The same Katie who had been publicly dumped like an old, ugly mattress.

Taking a deep breath, she dropped the basket to the floor, swung back to face Matt, and ordered, "Kiss me."

Chapter Two

"What?" Matt choked out. "Here? But—"

"Here and now," she hissed and pulled his head to hers.

It all happened so quickly, Matt had little time to react. Not that he would have refused her anyway. The odds of a strange woman coming up to him in a grocery store and demanding a kiss were about the same as the Red Sox's chances of winning the World Series. Slim to none. And the fact that the woman was as beautiful as this one only made the situation more intriguing.

Obliging her demands, but adding a few of his own, his mouth drifted over hers, and he tugged her closer. She wanted a kiss and she'd get one. He might be a lot of things, but he wasn't one to disappoint, not when it came to kisses. Or other bedroom sports.

He teased his tongue along the seam of her mouth, urging her for more, trying to satisfy the wave of desire that had slammed into him like a freight train when she'd grabbed him.

She arched against him, bringing the softness of her

breasts up to his chest. Flames erupted in his midsection, and for a moment, he forgot where they were.

"Katie?"

Matt's gaze jerked toward the sound of two voices. A tall man a few years younger than Matt had his arm draped over the hips of a blonde. Both their mouths gaped in perfect, shocked *O*s.

Although she ended the kiss, the woman in Matt's arms didn't pull away. "Oh my," she murmured, so softly he barely heard her, "so that's what it would be like."

Now that his head was in an upright position, he took a second to peruse his female body burglar. She was probably only five-foot-three, but what was packed into those sixty-three inches was exactly what he liked. She was slender, with a hint of curves under her loose-fitting tank and denim shorts. Her hair—long and the same honey-brown color as a good beer—fell loosely about her face in soft waves that made him remember exactly what kind of fun could be had in the back seat of his convertible.

She stroked his cheek and held his gaze, giving him the fleeting sensation of a long-time lover. Then, poised and in control, she turned and faced the twosome.

"Steve and Barbara, what a nice surprise." Her voice was filled with sweetness and sarcasm. Matt noticed her hands clench into tight fists, out of sight of the happy couple, but right over the contours of her very pleasing backside.

When his bike had broken down this afternoon, he'd thought returning to Mercy and staying at his parents' house was a mistake. He'd vowed to come back, show the town he had bucked their predictions and become a successful businessman, not a felon. So far, he'd had little time to do more than tangle with a woman in a banana suit, change his clothes, grab his old convertible and head to the store for the kind of food his mother refused to keep in her pantry.

And then, this woman, a pint-size ball of fire, had surprised the hell out of him and made his homecoming almost fun.

Matt watched with amusement as the trio exchanged uncomfortable, stumbled greetings. The tension in the air was thick and sticky, but all were masking it behind a polite facade. He presumed Steve, one of those guys with a boyish smile, was the "ex" and Barbara the mistress who had turned his head. The woman's kiss had probably been some sort of revenge.

Steve dropped his arm from the blonde's waist. "Katie, I didn't think that was you. I saw you…kissing and well…" his voice trailed off. He looked shocked.

"I guess you didn't know me that well after all, Steve." She hugged herself to Matt. He didn't complain.

"So, ah, how've you been?"

"Oh, fine. Business is booming. I couldn't be happier." She grabbed Matt's arm and plastered it to her side.

Matt couldn't help but take advantage. It was, after all, part of his baser nature. He stroked her waist with lazy movements that spoke of tangled sheets and spent passions. His hand glided down the soft cotton of her tank, along the fabric of her shorts, tracing her body. If she wanted Stevie Boy to think they were lovers, that was an easy, and enjoyable, part to play.

She wasn't going for an Oscar. She laced the fingers of her right hand with his, effectively stilling his hand and keeping it from straying anywhere interesting at all.

Spoilsport.

Whoever she was, this woman had lit a fire under him that wasn't being doused easily. A fire that was going to be visible to the whole world if he kept letting his thoughts run toward taking her to bed. Mentally, he recited the Pledge of Allegiance, cooling his ardor with a dash of patriotism. It worked—a little.

"Have you really been okay?" Steve moved forward.

Barbara grabbed his hand before he strayed too far. "Stevie, we're late for the party. They ordered the pay-per-view fight, you know. We'll miss the beginning." She tried to reel him back in, but didn't succeed.

He waved his hand to shush her, his gaze on Katie. "I'm glad things are going well," Steve said. "Since we moved to Michigan, I've lost touch with...everyone. Anyway, we drove down to Mercy today. We're only staying for a week, because, well, Barbara and I are getting married. Next Saturday. It's kind of last minute. We've barely told anyone yet so, I...I figured you might not have heard."

Matt glanced at Katie. Tears shone in her azure eyes. He saw her self-control eroding and cursed the man that could make a woman as beautiful as this one cry. She didn't deserve this humiliation.

"Congratulations, *Stevie*," Matt boomed, falling into the charade of being Katie's lover with gusto. "Katie and I are damned glad to hear your news." Matt clapped him hard on the shoulder.

Steve wobbled, then regained his balance. "Thanks." He rubbed his shoulder.

"When you meet the woman of your dreams, it all feels right, doesn't it?" He splayed his fingers across Katie's waist, and pressed a kiss to her hair. The sensual, warm scent of shampoo and sunlight wafted up to greet him. Her hair was velvet, falling in russet waves he pictured fanned out across his pillow. "Feels just right," he murmured.

Steve ignored Matt. "I wanted you to hear the news from me."

"I'm happy for you, Steve." Katie squared her shoulders and perked up in Matt's arms.

"You are?" He looked confused.

"Steve, that was a year ago. I've moved on. And after I met Matt, I forgot all about you." She flashed Matt a warm smile.

He was flabbergasted, not only by her smile, but that she knew his name. He'd only been in town for four hours. How did she know who he was? Was he that recognizable after an eleven-year absence? And why didn't he remember her?

Before he could give it another thought, Barbara piped in. "I guess the rumors aren't true, then."

"And what rumors are those?"

"That you're becoming…well, to put it plainly," she gave a little giggle, "a recluse, pouring everything into your shop." She shook her head, as if Katie's life were the saddest thing she'd ever encountered. "But after that, ah, very public display, I guess you have moved on. Why don't you introduce us to this new man in your life?"

"Matt Webster, my…my fiancé."

Matt swallowed. *Engaged?* This game was going too far for his tastes. Pretending to be a lover, now *that* he could do. And do very well. Pretending to be a future husband was way over the top. He needed to get out of here before he was saddled with an imaginary family and a St. Bernard.

"He is? You are?" Barbara didn't look as though she believed Katie's story. Matt saw a flare of jealousy in Barbara's gaze as it darted between Katie and Matt. "Well, I'm happy for you."

"Are you?"

"Well, sure." But the blonde didn't sound happy at all. Maybe she was the type who stole her friend's Barbies because they seemed nicer than her own. The grass, he'd found, was always greener when you looked at it with envy-colored eyes. Barbara turned to go, tugging Stevie Boy along with her.

"Oh, Barbara?" Katie called.

The blonde pivoted back. "What?"

"Make sure you have a ride home from the church. In case you're the only one who shows up."

Even though she knew it was spiteful, Katie took a small measure of satisfaction in Barbara's gasp and reddened face, mirrored by the nearby jars of spaghetti sauce. Barbara yanked Steve down the aisle, striding fast and furious toward the exit.

When they were gone, Katie let out a deep breath. What a way to change her image. Maul a stranger and then pretend she was engaged to him. In a town like Mercy, that kind of behavior was going to start a lot of talk. Talk that could get blown out of proportion, and set off a renewed stream of gossip. Had she made a mistake?

She was almost afraid to face Matt. Even though he'd gone along with her charade, he might not find the aftermath amusing.

Apparently a lot of other people did, Katie realized. Every minute of the exchange had been witnessed by a throng of people who had gathered at either end of the aisle. A half dozen shocked faces peeked around the spaghetti and ravioli, drinking in the sight of staid, predictable Katie Dole exchanging much more than pleasantries with a stranger and battling with her former bridesmaid beside the Chef Boyardee.

Alice Marchand, Katie's eighty-year-old neighbor, marched down the aisle. "Good for you, dear." She patted Katie's arm. "That Spencer boy and his floozy deserved every bit of that after what they did to you. Why, in my day, if a man left a woman at the altar, her daddy would get his shotgun and—"

"I'm sure my daddy considered that." Katie laughed.

"And you, young man, who are you?" Miss Marchand,

the toughest biology teacher ever to educate at Mercy High, lowered her spectacles and bent closer.

"Matthew Webster, ma'am."

She didn't look surprised. "Georgianne and Edward's boy?"

Matt nodded. So he was definitely *the* Matt Webster, Katie thought. Funny, he didn't look like a wild child. She couldn't imagine him married to Olivia, either. She seemed too…arctic and polished.

"You have a lot of gumption to come back. But it's good to see you home, where you belong." Miss Marchand nodded.

"Thank you, ma'am. I'm back for good," Matt said.

But that statement only started the crowd's titterings up again. "I think that's my cue to go, before they decide to lynch me," he said with a dry, bitter laugh. Then he took Katie's hand and brought it to his lips. When he kissed it, his gaze never left hers. The air between them crackled with sensuality and promise. "It was a pleasure to meet you. I do hope I see you again, Mystery Woman, and finish what we started. Soon."

Then he was gone, striding past the gaping townspeople, leaving Katie with a smile on her lips and a burning curiosity to know more about Matthew Webster.

Tools and parts were spread around Matt in an ever-multiplying circle as he dismantled his motorcycle and began the tedious repair job. His midnight-blue Chevy SS convertible, which had patiently waited under a tarp for the past eleven years, had miraculously started this afternoon. Someone had taken it in for service. The telltale sticker on the windshield said the Chevy had been in for an oil change two weeks ago.

Matt figured his mother had taken care of the car, though

he couldn't quite see her ordering up the lube special. Either way, the pampered auto had started easily, saving him from having to ask to borrow his father's Mercedes. He was back, but he wasn't up for a confrontation. Not yet. Using the motorcycle as an excuse, he'd taken a quick shower, avoiding his father, and then run into town for the parts he needed.

And run into one hell of an interesting woman, he mused, recalling her impetuousness and her kiss. She'd been hot and sweet at the same time, like the fireballs he'd eaten as a kid. He imagined drawing her closer, taking her into his arms, lowering the straps of her tank top down her shoulders, over the swell of her breasts....

The socket wrench slipped from his fingers and tumbled into his lap. Throbbing pain brought a quick halt to his fantasy.

He took a deep breath, trying to block the searing pain and focus on the motorcycle, not the girl. It wasn't easy. The fluid lines of the bike, the butter-softness of the leather seat, the sleek metal curves, all had him picturing the stranger named Katie and imagining her on the bike wearing nothing more than a smile.

This time, he managed to catch the wrench before it rendered him impotent.

"Matt, you're home!" His mother rounded the corner and entered the garage, a basket of freshly clipped yellow tulips in her hands. Georgianne Webster, her ash-blond hair in slight disarray from her trip to the garden, stood in the shadowed entryway clutching the basket like a lifeline, looking unsure.

"Hello, Mom." He scrambled to his feet and grabbed a rag. He wiped his hands several times, avoiding her gaze. After eleven years of nothing but letters, he felt self-conscious, clumsy.

"I saw you take the Chevy out earlier," she said.

"It started right up," he said. "Thank you for taking care of it and getting the oil changed."

"I didn't do that, Matt. Your father did."

"Oh." He let that thought digest for a minute. He grabbed the bouquet, thrusting the flowers at her. "These are for you. I know roses are your favorites and because it's April, yours won't be blooming for two more months…" he shrugged. "Anyway, I thought they'd cheer you up a little, since you've been so worried about Father." He leaned over and kissed her cheek.

When the familiar scent of her hit his senses, the full impact of how long he'd been gone slammed into him. He swallowed several times to get rid of the lump that had suddenly formed in his throat before he started acting like a blubbering idiot.

Without thinking, he drew his mother to him. The move popped the tension like a balloon burst by a pin. The basket clattered to the ground and she enfolded him in a fierce hug, not even noticing the flowers crushed between them.

"Oh Matthew, we've missed you," she whispered. Then she leaned back, cupping his face in her soft hands and studying him, as if searching for the Matt she knew. Tears trickled down her cheeks, tiny lines of emotion marring her makeup.

The feeling of home, of belonging, surged through him. That damned lump forced its way back into his throat. "Me too, Mom," was all he could manage.

"I'm so glad you're home." She wiped her eyes and took a half step back. "I guess the flowers got caught up in our reunion." Her laugh was shaky when she took the bouquet from him and buried her nose in their scent.

"It's okay, Mom. They're just roses."

"No, not just roses. Not when they're from you." She

added them to the basket, careful not to crush them further. "Remember the time you picked those daisies for me? You were seven, I think. The poor things were drooping like sad little puppies. But I kept them, pressed into the front of my Bible. They're still there, between Genesis and Exodus."

He chuckled. "If I remember right, you were pretty mad about those daisies. I'd yanked them out of Mrs. Rollins's garden and she complained."

"Eugenia Rollins was a cranky woman who couldn't appreciate a little boy showing his mother he loved her. I did have to give you a lecture, but your heart was in the right place."

"I'll keep that in mind on your birthday." Matt winked. "I noticed the neighbor's petunias are blooming."

"You're still incorrigible," she said softly, brushing a hand along his cheek. Her deep-green eyes were misty.

When he was younger, that word had been used to describe him more than once, especially by his father. It had practically become his middle name after he'd kidnapped a cow from Amos's farm and snuck it into the high school's gym the night before the Thanksgiving game. And the time he'd been caught driving his father's car—at fourteen and without a license. Not to mention the long list of smashed mailboxes and broken windows that littered his childhood résumé. But all that was over now.

"I've changed, Mom. For the better." And he had. It had been a long road to get there, but he'd made it, half dragging himself out of the depths of hell and back to the surface.

She searched his gaze, considering, evaluating. "I believe you have. I'm proud of you, Matt. It must have taken a lot of courage and strength, after what you went through."

Her face softened. In her eyes, he saw sympathy, an echo of his own pain. Images of that last night rocketed through him, fast, furious, hard. With a mental slamming of the door, he sealed that vault of memories. Their reunion was still a fragile thing, vulnerable to the past and he wasn't ready to face everything. Not yet.

"Will you be here for dinner?" she asked, clearly sensing his need for a change of subject.

"That depends. Are you making meat loaf?"

She laughed again, an easy, light sound. "You could have filet mignon and you're asking for my meat loaf?"

He shrugged. "I'm a man of simple tastes."

"All right. But it will have to be turkey meat loaf. It's healthier for your father."

Matt groaned. "Turkey is for Thanksgiving, not meat loaf." He pointed to the bag on the garage floor. "At least I made a pit stop for some good old-fashioned chili before I came home."

"Keep that away from your father," she admonished. "You know he can't resist chili." She kissed him on the cheek and started to lead the way into the house.

Matt cleared his throat. "How is Father?"

"He's recuperating pretty well. He's stubborn, though, and getting him to change hasn't been easy."

I know that firsthand. "Does he know I'm back?"

"Yes." She didn't say any more. Her silence about his father's reaction meant the years of separation hadn't changed much of anything. She paused at the top of the steps, then turned to him. "Why did you come back? It was more than your father's heart attack, wasn't it?"

He hesitated, forming the words in his head, finally giving voice to his own explanation. "To reclaim my life. I hit thirty and realized it was past time I grew up. Then Father got sick. It seemed the perfect time to start over. To come back."

"It was the right choice," she said. "It's not going to be easy, you know. Forgiveness doesn't come easy for some."

He knew she was talking about his father and Olivia. Hell, half the town saw him as a callous, irresponsible man who didn't deserve the life of privilege the Webster name had given him. But what they didn't know was how that name had made him suffer, and how impossible it had been to forgive himself.

"I didn't expect it would," Matt said, wondering if his return would be worth the price he'd be paying.

Katie kicked off her sneakers and placed the grocery bag on the counter. Popsicles went into the freezer, TV dinner was unwrapped and tossed into the microwave, cans were placed alphabetically in the cabinet. Within minutes, she was curled up on her sofa, picking at a plastic plateful of bland manicotti.

She reached for the remote control and flipped through the *TV Guide*. Two movies she had seen before and some woman-in-jeopardy special on channel seven. Television, or the books for the shop—already pored over a million times. *Gee, the real height of excitement in the middle of Indiana,* she thought.

She'd spent too much time cooped up here, worried about the shop and depressed about her non-wedding. She imagined herself, twenty years down the road, unkempt hair to her knees, wearing smelly, tattered clothes, muttering about what could have been if she hadn't been stood up at the altar. If she allowed the old Katie to wallow in self-pity for one minute more, she'd surely turn into Miss Havisham. And deep down inside, that's exactly what she feared would happen.

Maybe if she got out, networked a little, she could take care of both things at once. She might be dateless, but she was not the hermit Barbara had accused her of being.

Katie dashed into her bedroom, transforming her usual

self into what she hoped was someone who looked adventurous. She poufed her hair, painted her lips and slipped into a dress that wasn't exactly revealing, since her closet didn't contain anything that wasn't practical, but at least was more feminine than jeans.

Then she took a long, hard look at herself in the mirror, assessing the changes and resisting the urge to tamp down her hair and wipe off the lipstick. A day ago, a year ago, she would have. Katie had always lived her life plain and quiet. No longer. She took a deep breath, squared her shoulders and headed for the door before she could change her mind.

It was Friday night and the new Katie Dole was going out. Alone.

Matt sat on one of the silk-upholstered claw-foot chairs at the hand-carved mahogany dining-room table, under an elaborate three-tier crystal chandelier, surrounded by the finest china money could buy.

And wished he was lying on a blanket under the stars, with a cooler packed with fried chicken and sitting beside a beautiful honey-headed woman who really knew how to kiss.

"Hello, Matthew." His father's voice brought an abrupt halt to Matt's reverie.

When he saw him, Matt choked back a gasp. The rugged, hearty Edward he had left behind eleven years ago had been replaced by an old man with pale skin and tired eyes, shuffling across the room in a robe and slippers. Matt couldn't believe the damage a few clogged arteries had wreaked on a once-imposing, seemingly immortal man. For a second, Matt's resentment disappeared. He considered walking over to his father and ending the years of animosity with an embrace.

He was halfway out of his seat when his father said, "Have you seen Olivia yet?"

The mention of his ex-wife was like a stab to Matt's gut and his father knew it. Why had Matt hoped the heart attack and the years apart would make a difference? Nothing inside Edward had changed. Not a single thing. His heart was forged out of the same cold steel that was used to create the buildings he sold.

Edward folded his hands together and rested them on the table in front of him, a physical gesture Matt knew meant his father was getting down to business. Matt slowly sipped his water, waiting.

He watched his father rearrange his silverware until it was in a perfect line perpendicular to the table edge, and thought about the two traits he had inherited from Edward—tenacity and drive. Edward Webster had been penniless when he'd left his parents' home in Toledo at the age of eighteen. It had taken him seven years of selling commercial properties to save enough money to buy a part interest and the position of vice president in the floundering and grateful Corporate Services. Within two years, Edward owned the company and had renamed it Webster Enterprises.

Nearly three decades later, it was the largest, most profitable firm in the state. Edward had built it up with his own two hands. For that, Matt admired and respected him.

But Matt despised the underhanded way his father forced people to do his bidding. Edward Webster used every tool at his disposal—guilt, rage and humiliation—to bring others around to his way of thinking. That was a lesson Matt had learned personally. The night his father had turned on his own flesh and blood had wiped out whatever love and admiration Matt felt and had replaced it with simmering resentment.

"Matthew," his father said finally, "you should pay

Olivia a visit and try to patch things up. She never remarried, you know. She went back to her maiden name, but that doesn't mean everything is over between you two. People will talk about your return. There are a lot of questions that were never answered. Not for anyone, especially Olivia."

Matt had a few questions of his own for his ex-wife, but he didn't mention that to his father. "There's nothing to say, Father. Olivia and I haven't had so much as a conversation in a decade. Much like you and I."

Edward tore a fresh-baked roll in half and applied fat-free margarine in precise, economical movements. He said nothing.

"I have no plans to resurrect anything with Olivia. We won't be reconciling for the benefit of the country club."

"I don't give a damn about the country club," Edward exploded, slamming the butter knife down. "That girl is hurting. She needs you. I will *not* have a son of mine ignore his wife, ex or not, when she's still suffering from a horrible loss."

Matt popped out of his chair and placed both hands on the table. He leaned forward, his gaze leveled on his father's face. "You think she's the only one that suffered? *Do you? Do you* even consider how I might have felt? No, you think about how your son's actions might affect your social standing."

Edward leaned back in his seat. "That's not true."

"When I walked out that door eleven years ago, I was in more pain than you will ever know." Matt swallowed and willed the shudders of agonizing memories of that night to stop, prayed for the rage to replace the pain. "Do you remember what you said to me? 'Think about how this will look.'" Matt shoved his chair under the table and headed for the door. "That told me exactly how much you cared about *my* feelings, Father."

Matt stormed out and headed for the one place he knew would take the edge off his anger—a bar.

Chapter Three

Katie hopped onto a barstool at the Corner Pocket, Mercy's sole choice for evening entertainment, and tried to look cool and unaffected by her solitary status. It wasn't easy. It seemed every eye in the place, including those of the massive moose-head over the restroom door, was watching her.

I can do this. I can sit alone in a bar and not feel like a twenty-five-cent sideshow at the circus. Come see the Lonely, Bitter Old Maid—scariest creature this side of the Mississippi.

"Hey, Jim. How are you?" she said to the bartender, desperate for anyone to talk to.

"Pretty good, Katie. It's been a while since I've seen you here. Welcome back," said Jim Watkins, the rotund, friendly owner of the Corner Pocket. His open face and perpetual smile were encouraging and just what Katie needed. "Hey, I heard you got engaged. Congratulations."

For a second, Katie stared at him blankly. "Oh...oh that.

Well, I—'' What could she say? She decided to ignore it. In time people would talk about something else. "Thanks."

Katie drummed her fingers on the bar and glanced around the room. It was early yet and there were only a few people she knew here. Thankfully she noticed that Steve and Barbara were nowhere to be seen. They were probably cuddling somewhere, getting popcorn stuck in their teeth and watching Stone Cold Steve Austin wallop Hulk Hogan.

Jim placed a napkin before her. "What'll it be, Katie?" He laid a hand on the stack of glasses, waiting for her answer.

She was tempted to bolt out the door. Instead, she gripped the edge of the bar. "Umm...I don't know." She racked her brain for the name of a sophisticated drink, the kind ordered by women who ventured out alone. But she didn't know any. She rarely drank and usually nursed a draft Budweiser all night. She doubted a beer-foam mustache would make her look cool.

"Make it a tequila sunrise for the lady," said a voice from behind her. "And a...a Coke for me."

She spun around on the stool. Matt Webster. In the flesh and at her elbow. His eyes skimmed over the floral outfit, lingering just enough to let her know he approved. The breezy spring dress had been a good choice. A very good one.

Chalk up a point for the new Katie.

"I thought you might like something sweet but with a little bite to it." He grinned. "The total opposite of you, of course."

Put that resolution to work, Katie girl.

"You didn't find me sweet this afternoon?" She batted her eyelashes and did her best to look innocent.

"*Sweet* isn't quite the word that comes to mind when I think of you. And as for having a little bit of a bite," his

voice was low, dark, "well, you didn't let me get that far."
He was closer now, his breath warm on her face, his mouth
inches away. "*Fiery, spontaneous* and *bewitching* are better
adjectives for you."

"A tequila sunrise and a Coke for the happy couple,"
Jim announced, placing the glasses before them. Katie
jerked back, away from Matt, and felt heat rise to her face.

She wrapped her hands around the glass, marveling at the
way the drink mirrored its name. And how Matt looked as
though he'd stepped out of the pages of a magazine.
Granted, his leather jacket, white T-shirt and tight-fitting
jeans were from an issue of *Harley Rider* instead of *GQ*,
but the overall effect was the same. Enticing. Magnificent.
One-hundred-percent American male.

She swallowed hard and tried not to think about how
good he'd look in a tuxedo. That image was way too powerful. Her hormones were already raging. Picturing him in
evening wear would definitely be her undoing.

"What shall we drink to?" He raised his glass. His gaze
never left her face.

"To new beginnings."

He nodded. "Appropriate." He tapped his glass against
hers with a soft clink. She watched him drink. When his
lips met the rim, the powerful, gut-coiling memory of kissing him in the supermarket hit her.

"Celebrating your engagement?" Barbara's voice sliced
through the air with sarcastic precision. "Funny, no one else
in town knows about this wedding. How long *have* you been
dating?"

Katie froze. Putting on a ten-minute charade in the grocery store had been easy. A temporary game, not a life-
changing experience. Flirting with Matt in the dimness of
the bar was one thing; stepping away from who she'd been

for the last twenty-four years and slipping into an entirely new persona, in front of people she knew, was another.

"Katie and I have known each other for months," Matt said, saving her from a response. "We've just been long-distance lovers. Until now." He took Katie's hand, flashed her a wicked smile, and turned to face Barbara and Steve, who was bringing up the rear.

Barbara's gaze narrowed. "Then why didn't you get her a ring?"

Without missing a beat, Matt answered, "Because I'm having my great-grandmother's ring reset for Katie. She deserves something as special as she is."

Barbara harrumphed. "Katie always was lucky. In high school, it was grades. Now, she's a store owner and she has *you*." Her gaze roamed over Matt, making little secret of her desire. If he noticed, he didn't react.

This was a new twist. Barbara, who looked like Madonna and had never had trouble getting a man, was jealous of Katie for her grades? Her store? Had that spurred Barbara to steal Steve, the one thing Katie had that was stealable?—

"Anyway, Steve forgot to ask Katie something earlier," Barbara said. Steve shot Barbara a look of protest, but she nudged him with her elbow. "Go ahead."

He cleared his throat. "I still feel bad about the way things ended," he began. "You said there were no hard feelings and so, Barbara, well, I mean Barbara and I, want to invite you to the wedding."

"My father's managed to pull together quite a bash on short notice," Barbara said. "We're going to have—"

"You stood me up *at the altar* in front of half the town to run off with my bridesmaid and now you want me to come to your wedding?"

Matt put a hand on her arm and leaned to whisper in her ear. "It might be a good idea to go," he whispered in her ear.

"Are you insane?" she whispered back.

"It would be a hell of a way to get closure." He grinned.

This man could read her like a book. He'd pushed the right button, the one that triggered her compulsion to show the town she'd moved on, despite what Steve had done to her. But go to their wedding? Wasn't that a bit much?

Then she thought about seeing Steve squirm in front of the minister, if he made it that far this time, of seeing Barbara eat her words about Katie being a recluse. And then there was the store—a bit of talk might spur some business. This was an opportunity, not an insult.

She turned to Barbara and Steve. "We'd love to come. *Both of us.*" The new Katie was brave, but she wasn't quite up to doing this alone.

Barbara's mouth dropped open. "Both of you? How wonderful. It will be so nice to have one of the Websters at our wedding," she said.

"What a coup," Matt said dryly.

Steve eyed Matt. "You aren't planning on pulling one of your famous stunts at the reception, are you?"

"And just what is that supposed to mean?"

"I know who you are." He leaned into Matt's face, his voice low. "You tore up this town when you lived here, and you got arrested so many times, the sheriff had to hire a deputy just to keep an eye on you."

"Yeah, well I'm older and wiser now. And a lot bigger."

Katie saw the storm brewing between the two men. She scooted off the stool, grabbing up a handful of darts from the dish on a nearby table. She put a hand on Matt's shoulder and tugged him away from Steve. "Come on, play darts with me."

Matt backed up and accepted the darts she handed him. "I think that's a good idea." His gaze never wavered from Steve.

"We were on our way to the dining room to pick up some

pizzas for the fight anyway.'' Barbara grabbed Steve's hand and started leading him toward the swinging door that separated the two halves of the Corner Pocket.

"One more thing.'' Steve pivoted back to Matt. "Katie's a good person. Don't hurt her.'' Then he walked away, leaving Katie stunned. Barbara was jealous of her? Steve was being protective? Had the world just turned upside down?

Then Barbara called over her shoulder, "See you next Saturday,'' and the world flipped upright again.

"I wouldn't miss it for anything,'' Katie grumbled.

When the door swung shut behind the couple, Matt released a gust of air. "A few years ago, I would have knocked a guy like that clear across the bar, just for the hell of it.''

"And why didn't you today?''

"I'm not who I used to be.''

"Well, that makes two of us.'' She smiled. "Thanks for coming to my rescue. Again.''

"It was my pleasure. Both times.''

"I don't usually kiss strangers at the corner grocery,'' she said. "I was trying to…''

"Make him jealous?'' Matt supplied.

"No, not jealous. I wanted him to see I've gone on with my life.''

"And have you?''

"Of course.'' That was mostly a lie. All Katie knew now was she didn't want to go back to who she was before, no matter how safe and comfortable it felt.

Matt twirled a dart between his fingers. "I don't want to be mean, but what did you see in him in the first place?''

Katie snorted. "The better question is what did he see in me? I was the class geek, complete with the glasses and the physics books. He was the captain of the football team.''

"Let me guess. You tutored him in geometry?''

She let out a laugh. "Algebra.'' Something about the

chase, or the bonus of good grades, had kept Steve with her throughout high school. She'd been the one who could have used a tutor—in how not to be fooled by the illusion of a relationship. Steve had dumped her at graduation—for the hot cheerleader who'd given him the time of his life under the bleachers.

"You're a beautiful woman, you know," Matt said. "You probably could have had any guy in high school."

"They weren't exactly lining up for dates."

"Well, they were stupid."

She shook her head. "I was the stupid one. I went away to college and when I came home, Steve was there. He told me I was good for him, that being with me kept him from getting into trouble. I guess he believed that, too. Maybe I had an extra-bad case of homesickness or jet lag or something, because I took Steve back, even knowing he'd cheated on me. I was still half in love with those high-school memories. Mostly, though, I was half idiot. I believed him when he said he wanted to marry me and be faithful. I thought he'd changed." She scowled. "A bona fide Oprah moment."

Matt gestured toward the door to the restaurant. "And that's when Babs there came into the picture?"

Katie dropped her gaze to the darts in her hand. "On my wedding day, no less. He sent me a letter afterwards that summed up all my shortcomings and defended his choice of Barbara."

Matt cursed under his breath. "I ought to—"

"Don't. It's over, in the past." She fidgeted with the darts. "Anyway, thanks again for helping me out."

"Are you trying to get rid of me?" He moved closer, a breath away. She could feel the warmth of his body, smell the scent of leather mixed with musky cologne.

"Should I? After what I've heard, maybe it would be in

my best interests." Katie's heart began racing at triple-speed, her pulse hammering through her veins.

It was as if a rocket had launched itself in her midsection. She'd wanted a little spice in her life—a dash of pepper, maybe—not a truckload of red-hot chilies roaring through her at the speed of light. He was too handsome, too desirable and way too dangerous. She would be crazy to get involved with him. He seemed to be a lot more than even the new Katie could handle.

"Don't you feel the connection between us?"

"A single kiss doesn't make us soul mates," she countered. Each breath caught in her throat. The memory of that encounter, and all its deeper implications, still quivered within her.

"If it were an ordinary kiss." He traced along the edge of her bottom lip and she inhaled, resisting the urge to taste the tip of his finger, to do much, much more. "Which that most certainly wasn't."

"No, it wasn't." She wanted him to touch her, kiss her again. Anything to assuage the strange and furious storm inside.

"Who are you?" he asked softly, his deep blue gaze boring into hers. "An angel sent to tame me or a devil to tempt me?"

"Neither," she murmured. Heat radiated from his body, charging the air between them. Her breasts were taut, the nipples puckered against the confines of her bra. She chanced a glance downward and saw that Matt was in the same state as she. That knowledge, that power, sent a thrill straight through her.

"If we're going to get this close," he said, watching where her gaze went, "I think I should at least know your least name."

"You…you already do."

"I think I might have remembered that tidbit. A beautiful

woman ravages me in the spaghetti aisle and I definitely wouldn't forget her first or last name.''

''I didn't ravage you!''

''Honey, if I'd been a side of beef, there wouldn't have been much more than bones left after you got through with me.''

She laughed and the sound of it broke the simmering tension for a moment. ''A bit of an exaggeration, don't you think?''

''Perhaps. But until we get a chance to finish what we started,'' he said, tracing a finger along the outline of her jaw and starting that fire roaring all over again, ''we'll never know the truth about your ravaging skills, now will we?''

She couldn't answer. Heck, she could barely breath when he did that.

''So tell me, Mystery Kissing Bandit, what's your last name?''

''Do you remember running into a piece of fruit this morning?''

It took him a second to make the connection. ''*You're* the banana?''

She nodded. ''When I'm not going around kissing strange men, I masquerade as fruit for kicks,'' she said, amazed at her ability to exchange witty remarks. It had to be the tequila that had emboldened her—because the real Katie would have had her tongue tied in double knots.

''My, my, Katie Dole, you surprise me more every minute I know you.'' His gaze ran over her face, lingering on her lips. ''I'm not often surprised by women.''

''That's me, a surprise a minute.'' *What a complete lie. I couldn't surprise a cow.* She needed to change the subject, to give herself a second to think. She was playing a game where the rules were foreign and where Matt had the upper hand. ''We were about to play darts, remember?''

''I'd much rather play something else.''

"Darts is all you're going to get tonight," she said. "So work out your frustrations on the bull's-eye."

"Let's raise the stakes. Loser takes the winner to dinner."

"Deal." Yesterday, she would have backed down from the challenge, would have run when she encountered a man with such dangerous sex appeal. But now, she was determined to hold her own against him—at least in darts.

It should be an easy bet, she reasoned. A girl didn't grow up with four brothers and not learn a thing or two about competing in barroom sports.

Katie stood on the line a few feet from the board, holding the gold-and-teal dart between her thumb and forefinger. She sighted the bull's-eye over the feathers and took aim.

As soon as the dart left her fingers, she knew the launch was wrong. Matt was two feet away, watching her from the sidelines and wreaking havoc with her concentration.

The dart landed in the ignominious outer circle. Zero points. Katie squinted at the board and redoubled her concentration. She threw the other two darts at the board. One landed in the ten-point spot, the other flew wide of the board and hit the wall.

"Might I offer a suggestion?" Matt said.

"I know how to shoot darts. I don't need any lessons." She stalked over to the board and ripped her darts out, knowing all the while that their placement said otherwise.

When she was safely behind the painted white line on the floor, he aimed his dart and let it go. It sailed smoothly into the bull's-eye. With resounding thwaps, the other two followed.

He was good. Better than she was. "All right. Show me what you know and save me the cost of feeding you when I beat you with your own techniques," she conceded.

"How much time do you have? *I* have all night."

The innuendo in his voice made flames rush to her

cheeks. "I've got five minutes. That should be more than enough time for you to teach me all you know."

"Good one." Another smile. He led her over to the line. Then he sidled up behind her, raising her right hand beside his.

The heat from his body, inches away, was incredible. She forced herself to stand steady, to resist the urge to back up and melt against his chest—and all his other desirable parts. The sexual charges detonating throughout her body were new, completely unexpected, and nearly consuming in their power over her mind.

"When you aim, be sure to oversight it a little. That compensates for the flight arc," he was saying. "Let me show you." He took her hand and placed a dart between her fingers. Then he rocked her hand back and forth, as if they were shooting the dart. "Keep it steady and remember, it's all in the wrist."

"Thanks. I will," she exhaled on a shaky breath. *Concentrate. On the darts.*

This time, she focused on the dartboard and blocked Matt from her mind. *Thwap, thwap.* Two hit the bull's-eye, the third landed on thirty points.

When it was his turn, she moved into place behind him. Just as he took aim, she purposely brushed her breasts against his back. The feel of him, of the simple intake and exchange of air that made his back slip along her chest, was intoxicating. Wanton need, so foreign to Katie, pounded through her veins.

For the first time in her life, she felt alive. Invigorated. Completely, totally feminine. "I, ah, wanted to get a closer look at your technique."

Matt's dart flew wide of the mark and landed with a thunk in the wall.

"You missed. What a shame."

"Pity, isn't it?" He glanced over his shoulder at her, his

gaze telling her he knew exactly what she was up to and that he was enjoying every minute of it.

And, if she admitted the truth, so was she. She felt bold, brazen, ready to take on any challenge.

"So, are you going to go?" Matt sent another dart sailing into the board.

"Where?" she asked, confused.

"To that wedding."

Any challenge but that one. "I don't know." Katie walked to the bar and took a drink. "I'm not up to watching one of my former friends marry the guy who left me at the altar."

"But you did say you'd go. With me." He sent his third dart into the board, hitting the bull's-eye.

"Not everyone keeps their promises."

"You seem the type of woman who would," he said softly, watching her, assessing her, peering into her soul. "And you did promise them we'd both go."

"I certainly don't expect you to carry this charade that far." She crossed to the line and waited for him to remove his darts. He did, then gestured that it was her turn to shoot. "You've done enough already."

"I haven't done *nearly* enough." He moved into place behind her. Her pulse quickened, racing along faster than the rabbit-hungry greyhounds on the big-screen TV across the room.

"If you went to the wedding," he continued in that teasing, tempting voice that was probably the same one the snake had used on Eve, "with a man who is obviously crazy about you at your side," his breath was warm against her neck, "it would show Steve you were a prize he never should have given up."

The air stood still. "Where am I going to get a guy like that?"

He spun her gently around to face him. "Right here."

"Why would you do that for me? You don't even know me."

He paused. "It would be a bargain of sorts. I'll pretend to be your fiancé and in return, you help me. You took a chance on me in the grocery store. Come on, take another one now."

She cocked her head. "You'd do that, pretend you love me?"

"With pleasure."

"Why?"

"Because I need you as much as you need me." He flicked up the lapels of his leather jacket. "And because nothing can change a good girl's reputation like a bad boy."

This was the perfect solution. Matt would pretend to be her fiancé, ending the looks of pity and gossip that had been running around town for the past year. She'd have a chance to rewrite her image, dispelling Steve's declarations that she was boring and about as sexy as a dishtowel. And maybe, in the end, the store would be the winner. The business side of her said this was a way into the Webster home. A good deal all around. Wasn't it?

Did she dare to agree?

She studied him, reading a warmth in his eyes that was far from devilish. There was clearly more to this man than most people assumed. "You may dress like a bad boy," she said, "but inside, I think you're actually a good man."

A shade dropped over his face. "You don't know me very well."

"I think that's about to change, Matt Webster." She took a breath and thrust out a hand. "You have a deal."

Katie Dole, the straitlaced owner of A Pair of Posies, had just made a pact with the devil of Mercy.

Chapter Four

Twenty minutes later, they'd grabbed a table for two. Matt had a new Coke, but Katie refused a second tequila sunrise and stuck to nursing her first one. She twirled her half-empty glass on the smooth laminate tabletop. "What kind of help are we talking about? Exactly?"

The pose didn't fool him. She looked worried, even a bit scared. She'd agreed hastily, and Matt could see Katie was having second thoughts. A number of them. So far, he'd delayed telling her anything more about the "deal" they'd made until he'd figured it out for himself. He didn't know what had pushed him to offer the arrangement, just that he wanted a way to solve her problem...and a way to keep her near him just a little longer.

"Exactly?" he parroted while he scrambled for an answer.

"Please tell me what I've gotten myself into."

And then, finally, an idea came to him. Not the best idea, but one nonetheless. "I need help of the physical kind."

She raised her hands, warding him off. "I didn't agree to anything like *that*."

"My, my, Katie Dole. You do have a one-track mind." Although if he'd been pressed, he'd have to admit he'd just been imagining all kinds of interesting scenarios with her, him and his Harley. All without clothes. All in poses that would have made the *Kama Sutra*'s author blush. He may have changed his wild ways, but he hadn't become a monk.

Her face flushed a deep red. An attractive color on her, he mused. "I mean…well…you know."

"I have no idea what you're talking about." He affected a blank look.

"I don't—"

"The help I need doesn't involve a bed, I promise." He touched her arm to console her. But the shock of feeling that rippled through his veins had him wishing he'd proposed a very different sort of deal. "Are you busy in the morning?"

She visibly relaxed. "No. The shop doesn't open until ten. Sarah works until two so I have all morning free."

He wanted to touch her again, to feel her soft skin beneath his palm, but didn't. He corralled his thoughts into safer territory. "I'll pick you up at six. That's 6:00 *a.m.* And we'll see if you're as good with tools as you are with darts."

"Tools?"

"I'm not saying another word. Wear old clothes and be ready to work." She eyed him suspiciously but didn't say anything more. Matt nodded toward her drink. "Sure you don't want another one?"

"Oh, no." She pushed the glass away. The grenadine had already settled to the bottom, turning the sunrise into a sunset. "One more and I'll be on the bar, singing show tunes."

He chuckled. "That I've got to see sometime."

"It's not a pretty sight. I can't carry a tune to save my

life.'' She slid the cherry off the plastic sword in her drink and popped it into her mouth, veering Matt's mind off course for a minute. "Even got kicked out of choir when I was a kid because I kept disrupting the performance with my Alfalfa impersonations." She waggled the plastic sword at him. "Just don't ask me to sing 'The Star Spangled Banner' and we'll get along fine."

He laughed heartily. Being with this woman was good for him. She made him forget about his past, about facing it now that he was back. He was looking forward to tomorrow as eagerly as a child waiting for the last bell of the school year. He hadn't felt this kind of anticipation in years. Too many years.

"I'll vouch for her singing," said a voice over his shoulder. "She's truly terrible."

Matt turned and saw the blond woman who'd sold him the flowers that morning. She'd been behind the counter earlier and he hadn't noticed that she was pregnant. But now he did.

Her belly was round, large with the child she carried, and her face was smiling, happy. When he looked at her, though, he saw another woman's face, another birth, remembered cradling another baby in his arms.

She rubbed her belly in a circular, protective motion. Just like Olivia used to. Pain ricocheted through him, dispelling his happy, light mood like a winter nor'easter obliterating the autumn landscape. In his mind, he saw the tiny fingers, miniature toes and trusting face of the baby who had depended on Matt to keep him safe.

And Matt had failed. Failed in the worst possible way to protect his child. Failed to be the father he'd promised he'd be when the nurse had placed his son in his arms. At the one moment when his child needed him most, he'd been drowning himself in tequila.

The baby, whom he'd stopped naming in his mind because that made the pain unbearable, had paid the ultimate price for Matt's mistake. And every day since, Matt wished it had been him instead.

Katie's glass was inches away from his hand. Thirst parched his throat, not for the drink, but for the numbing effect of the alcohol. He hesitated, his hand hovering near the solace, the blissful blankness the glass could give him.

He could drink that one and another and another. And then the pain would dull, leaving him at peace for the short while that alcohol controlled his mind.

The glass was so close.

Inches from his grasp.

One sip. Just one.

Katie had called him a good man. Her words had slammed into him and hit right at his heart with more accuracy than any dart she could have thrown. He wasn't and he knew it, but her simple quiet comment had gotten under his skin. With a Herculean effort, he pushed the glass farther away and guzzled his soda instead.

Then he tucked those memories deep inside his mind and forced himself back to the present. To Katie.

"Took my advice, I see," the woman was saying, smiling at Katie.

"Only the going out part. He," Katie pointed a thumb at Matt, "happened to be here."

"And who is he?" A man carrying a frothy mug of beer and a bubbling glass of ginger ale came up and stood between Sarah and Katie. Well over six feet tall, barrel-chested and with the same deep chestnut hair as Katie, the man put the drinks down and extended his hand. "Jack Dole," he said. "Brother to Katie and husband to Sarah."

"So you better watch out," the two women added simultaneously, bursting into laughter.

"He's been using that line for years," Katie explained. "He thinks it makes him sound all menacing and protective." Katie gave her brother a good-natured jab. "Now that he's part of the Mercy P.D., he gets paid to act that way."

Matt recognized Jack from high school. Jack had been quarterback of the football team; Matt had lettered in skipping school. The menacing looks Jack kept shooting his way told Matt he'd been recognized, too.

He didn't blame Jack one bit. If the roles had been reversed, Matt wouldn't have allowed a man with a reputation like his to share the air with his sister.

"Come on, let's grab a bigger table." Sarah took Matt's arm and propelled him toward a circular table surrounded by a quartet of chairs. "You might as well join us and see if you pass inspection."

"Inspection?"

"Jack makes it his personal mission to check out any men who get within ten feet of his baby sister," Katie answered. "As the oldest, he thinks he's the watchdog. Especially now that he's the only one in Mercy. Mark and Luke live in California and own their own software company. Nate's a Marine, so he could be anywhere."

Matt remembered a couple of the Dole boys from high school. They'd all been football-player size. "Were they a little short on genes when they got to you?"

"Ha, ha. Very funny. I'm not short, anyway. I'm just altitudinally challenged."

"Very P.C.," he said, chuckling. He pulled out a chair for her and slid it into place after she sat down. "So you're the youngest?"

"Yep. And the spoiled one, if you ask my brothers." Katie slid one leg over the other, giving Matt a quick flash of creamy skin before he took the seat beside her. "Jack was the one who spent hours combing his wiffle cut on the off chance Sarah might be stopping by to study with me. He was totally head over heels for her, but didn't have a clue how to show it.''

The former football hero of Mercy High, who'd once scored four touchdowns in a single game, turned beet-red.

"A common male deficiency," Sarah quipped.

Matt rested his arm along the back of Katie's chair. He resisted the temptation to let his fingers dangle down and drift across the top of Katie's shoulder. "When I'm interested in someone, she knows it.''

"Does that happen a lot?" Jack leaned forward. "You getting interested in someone?"

"A fair amount," Matt answered vaguely. Jack already had his hackles up, no sense adding fuel to the fire.

Jack lowered his voice, leaned a bit closer. "I hope my sister isn't going to be another notch on your belt.''

"Jack!" both women exclaimed.

"That's not what I'm after.''

"Good. Katie doesn't need another jerk. She deserves better.''

Better than me, you mean. "You're right.''

"Glad to hear we're on the same wavelength.'' He drained his beer. "Come on, Katie. Let's grab another round.''

Katie followed her brother to the bar, her cheeks on fire. Once they were out of earshot of Matt, she said, "I know what you're going to say, and I want to remind you that I can make my own decisions.'' He started to protest, but she put a hand over his mouth. "Stop.'' He opened his mouth to speak again. "No, I mean it. Jack, you're my brother and I love you, but I wish for once you'd realize I'm a grownup.''

"I know that, Katydid," he said, slipping into the familiar nickname of her youth. "I just don't want to see you hitching yourself to another guy who's trouble. I knew Matt in high school. He's not the kind of guy you bring home to meet Mom. I think—''

"Jack, don't. You, Nate, Mark and Luke all have a habit of leaping into my life and offering your opinions whether I ask for them or not." She knew he did it out of love but it was annoying all the same. "Remember Colin Parker, the boy who wanted to take me to the junior prom? Before he even asked me, you four knew everything about him, right down to his shoe size. You scared the poor guy off with all your questions, and you made me think he was some freak of nature because he wore a size-thirteen sneaker."

Jack laughed. "We're just looking out for our little sister.''

"Who happens to be twenty-four now," she reminded him. "Jack, I really don't need you to give me a report on who Matt Webster is. Let me figure that out on my own."

"But, Katie—''

"Is my husband interfering in your life again?" Sarah slid onto the stool beside Katie. She planted a kiss on Jack's cheek. "You have a heart of gold, honey, but you tend to be a tad overprotective." She smiled and Katie could feel their love flow into the space between them. "Now, why don't you go over there and get to know the new man in Katie's life?"

Jack scowled, but took his beer and followed his wife's request. A moment later, the two men sauntered over to the dartboard.

"I wouldn't call Matt the new man in my life, Sarah."

"I think you should start. Everyone else here thinks that."

Katie glanced around and saw several people casting looks at Matt, then at her, their eyebrows raised in surprise. A few women nodded their approval of Katie's choice when she met their gaze. Others squinted disapproval. She'd finally gotten a reaction other than pity. People weren't feeling bad for left-at-the-altar Katie anymore.

"Matt has caught the eye of every woman in this room," Sarah said, interrupting Katie's thoughts, "but he still comes back to you. The guy is absolutely captivated." She leaned forward. "So, are you going to go for it? Date him?"

"I'm not sure," Katie answered, not mentioning the agreement she and Matt had just made. "He's got quite the reputation."

"Yeah, but he's all grown up now and handsome as the devil."

That he was, Katie had to admit, watching Matt sling another dart at the board. "And just as tempting."

"A little temptation never hurt anyone. Besides, didn't you resolve to live a little?"

"Yes, but he might be more living than I can handle. Jack says—"

"Jack's a good man, but he doesn't know beans about the kind of guy who will make you happy," Sarah said. "I see something in this guy. I can't quite put my finger on it, but I know there's something worth saving there, no matter what his story is." Sarah laid a hand on her shoulder. "Give him a chance."

Sarah was right. Katie knew firsthand that rumors could blur the truth until it was unrecognizable. The real Matt, who had suffered the loss of a marriage and a baby, might be completely different from what she'd heard. She nodded. "One chance, then."

"It'll be enough," Sarah said. "He seems like a man who needs one."

Katie's gaze slid to Matt. Was he still the man he used to be? The rebel who had been—and still was—the talk of the town?

Or was he a man worth saving, as Sarah had said? And if so, was the new Katie strong enough to go through with their deal, no matter the consequences?

"I can't. Really, I can't." The morning sun had yet to rise and the birds were still cooing in their nests when Matt showed up on Katie's doorstep at six o'clock sharp.

To his surprise, she had been waiting for him, dressed in a pair of stonewashed jeans and a soft blue T-shirt that glided loosely over her torso. Such simple clothes, but when she wore them, they gave her a look of comfort, as if he could wrap himself around her and ease into peace.

But right now, she was backing all the way up to the top of the stoop and looking anything but relaxed. "Matt, I can't."

"Why not?"

"I've never been on a motorcycle before." She pointed at his Harley. She chewed on her upper lip. "I don't think I'm the kind of person who rides a—what do you call it—a...a hog?"

Laughter burst out of him. "Yeah, that's the bikers' term for it. I prefer Jane."

"You named your bike Jane?"

"Yep. Once you ride her, you'll know exactly how Tarzan felt when he swung through the jungle. There's nothing like it in the world. Riding a motorcycle is the closest thing to true freedom I've ever known." He patted the black leather seat. "Try it."

"I don't know."

"I thought you were looking for a little adventure to spice up your life."

"How did you know that?"

"Katie, I may not know you all that well, *yet,*" he saw her catch her breath at his implication, "but I get the distinct feeling that you aren't normally the type who dresses up as a banana, kisses strange men in the grocery store and then ventures out to a bar alone for a rousing game of darts."

"Well, no, not really."

"Then what are you doing all that for?"

She fidgeted with the porch railing. "I needed a change in my life. I've spent twenty-four years being predictable and conventional. *Boring.*"

"Is that what Steve told you in that letter?"

The look in her eyes told him he'd hit the truth. "Do you have a second career as a psychic?"

"Nope. I've just gotten pretty good at reading other people. When you work with a bunch of guys on a roof, you learn to spot the ones who are terrified of falling off and the hungover ones who are more likely to hammer their thumb than the nail. I need men I can trust on my crew. I had to figure out which ones those were before I hired them."

She smiled. "Are you trying to tell me I wouldn't be good on a roof?"

"You'd be good anywhere."

A blush crept into her cheeks and she looked away.

He gestured to the bike and tucked a challenge into his voice. "If you're not up to riding Jane," he slid a hand along the seat, "then I can go back and get my car instead."

Katie lifted her chin, slipped into a sweater and headed down the stairs. "It may be my first day of living dangerously," she said, "but I'm still wearing a helmet."

He chuckled. "Let me introduce you. Katie, this is Jane. Jane, this is Katie," he said, patting the bike seat. "Be nice because it's Katie's first time on a Harley."

Katie slid a hand down the leather seat, imagining Matt astride that seat, picturing herself squeezed into the space behind him. The fear of falling off the bike and tumbling headlong onto the concrete disappeared. What she feared most now was how riding behind him, their bodies pressed together like two pieces of bread, would make her feel.

He unhooked a black helmet from the back and handed it to her. "Here."

She thanked him and undid the chinstrap, trying not to focus on the seat. And Matt. And her and Matt on that seat.

"Katie Dole, is that you?"

Katie turned, the helmet halfway to her head, and saw Alice Marchand, who lived at the end of the block, heading toward her. A portly brown miniature dachshund attached to a rhinestone-beaded leash waddled alongside her mistress, an air of superiority in her upturned nose and spiked tail. Another neighbor, Colleen Tanner, was bringing up the rear, putting all her weight and sixty-plus years into keeping a tall, lean and hungry-looking Doberman from dragging her away. The Doberman strained at the leash—in the opposite direction of Miss Tanner.

Katie stifled a burst of laughter. The Misses, as they were called in the neighborhood, wouldn't take kindly to anyone poking fun at their wayward dogs.

"Are you getting on that brain-smasher?" Miss Marchand lowered her glasses and wrinkled her nose in reproach. "You must have a few screws loose to ride that contraption."

"We're just going for a slow cruise through town, Mrs. M. Katie will be perfectly safe," Matt replied. He knelt down to pet the dachshund, scratching behind her velvet ears. The little dog cuddled against his knee, lapping up the attention. Ten seconds later, the dog had settled onto the pavement, content and asleep.

Miss Marchand harrumphed and shook her head at the bike. "I came down here to offer my congratulations. I overheard you in the Sav-a-Lot, saying you two were engaged.

I don't know if you meant it to go public, but the news about you two has spread all over town. Why, I even heard the girls talking about it in Flo's Cut and Go yesterday afternoon.''

"You did?'' Katie gulped. That fast?

"Katie, this is Mercy. If there's anything the people here are good at, it's talking about everyone else. They all want to know how you kept Matt a secret all this time and why—''

"I know you,'' Miss Tanner interrupted. She'd finally managed to drag her dog over. "You're that Matt Webster.''

The Doberman escaped her grasp and began nosing Katie.

"We met at the wedding. Your *first* one.'' She shook her head, disapproval etched into her lips. "I told my niece she was making a mistake by marrying you. I knew you'd amount to trouble.''

The Doberman, now unattended, jumped on Katie's chest and began licking her face. She pushed at the dog, trying to get him down, but he only grew more persistent, as if he'd mistaken her for a steak. Miss Tanner was oblivious to her dog's actions, her attention riveted on Matt.

"Colleen, you're being awfully harsh.'' Miss Marchand shook her head. "And Katie doesn't need to hear this.''

"Oh, yes she does. He left Olivia.'' Miss Tanner eyed Matt with disdain. "Left her to fend for herself.''

"I left her with a hefty divorce settlement.'' Matt reached out, grabbed the big dog's collar, tugged him away from Katie and into a sitting position. The Doberman turned his head, looking very surprised that someone had actually stopped him from being bad, and stayed put. Thank goodness the dog's horrendous breath was no longer in Katie's face.

"Olivia needed you,'' Miss Tanner retorted.

"She had me. She didn't really want me to begin with.''

"I heard all about you and none of it was good." She turned to Katie. "You'd do well to stay away from this man, particularly as a woman with a business in this town."

"Colleen! You can't believe—or repeat—everything you hear, especially in a small town." Miss Marchand patted Matt's arm. The Doberman, apparently seeing this as an opportunity, raced over and began slobbering all over Matt's hand. "Give the man a little breathing room before you condemn him. You too, Sweet Pea," she said to the dog.

Katie saw Matt's eyebrows arch and his eyes widen. His mouth dropped open but not a sound came out. Clearly he hadn't expected Miss Marchand to come to his defense. The older woman leaned closer to Matt. Her deep pink dress flapped around her knees in the spring breeze, like a sheet pinned to a clothesline.

"You always came to my class. I never knew why. I thought perhaps you had an appreciation for flora and fauna." She shrugged. "Now, be a dear and put to rest a question that's been nagging this old woman for years. Why *did* you attend my class and skip all the others?"

"You encouraged me. In the things I really wanted to do." He said the words casually, as if it wasn't any big deal, but Katie got the opposite impression. "You helped me enroll in that after-school construction program. You said I shouldn't be ashamed of making my living with my hands because it was honest work."

"And did you make a living out of building things?"

"I own the second-largest construction company in Pennsylvania."

Miss Tanner snorted. "Sure you do."

Miss Marchand smiled and patted his arm again, narrowly avoiding the eager Doberman's tongue. "I knew you'd be successful. You just needed a push in the right direction."

"A shove was more like it," Matt replied. "I've always wanted to thank you, Miss Marchand."

"You just did, my dear." She turned and gave a short tug on the dachshund's leash. She awoke with a start and hopped to her feet. "Come on, Colleen. Let's finish our morning constitutional and leave these youngsters alone."

"But—"

"Colleen, you said your piece. Now let's walk down to Ray's Donut Shop. You know a donut always helps settle your stomach after you get all riled up."

"A donut does sound good," Miss Tanner conceded. She looked around for her dog and finally noticed him trying to gobble Matt's hand. "Sweet Pea! Come on, baby, let's go get you a cruller." The dog's ears perked up and he bounded over to his mistress, nearly toppling her.

Miss Marchand turned to Katie. "I still think getting on that thing is asking for trouble, dear," she said. She gave her hand a squeeze. "But I have a feeling Matt will watch out for you."

"I think you're right." Katie had always liked Miss Marchand, but after what had just transpired, she now admired her, too.

Matt stood silently beside Katie, twirling his helmet in his hands. In his gaze, Katie saw traces of wonder. Clearly, she wasn't the only one surprising the people of Mercy.

Chapter Five

After the Misses were gone, the street was quiet, save for the barking of a neighbor's poodle and the soft chirps of morning birds. Pretty houses lined Cherry Street, neatly tended lawns enclosed by picket fences. A picture-perfect small town, where unfortunately, memories lasted longer than the stone monument of Lewis and Clark in the park.

That reality suddenly hit Katie. By agreeing to this "deal" with Matt—a very public deal—she might have placed herself—and the store—in the middle of a quandary. A Pair of Posies needed Olivia Maguire's business. Needed it badly. Already, the whole town had probably heard about her "engagement." How would the ex-wife part of Olivia take that news? There seemed to be a lot of animosity there, if Miss Tanner was any indication.

Had her plan for a little revenge on Steve and Barbara ruined everything?

"Olivia is your ex-wife?"

"Yes." Matt slipped on his helmet and fastened the

straps. He seated himself on the motorcycle easily, comfortably.

"And?" Katie strapped her helmet on, then settled herself into the small space behind him.

"And she's one of my least favorite subjects. It's been over between us for a long time."

Maybe it was over for Olivia, too. Surely, they were all grownups. Katie's involvement with Matt, if that's what it was, shouldn't upset that apple cart too much.

"Does she—" Katie stopped when Matt cut her off.

"I'd rather not talk about her." He flipped up the kickstand and straightened the bike. His hand hovered over the ignition. "Not right now, not with you pressed up against me. I'd much rather concentrate on how nice *that* feels."

She scooted closer, drawn by primitive need. Her body had a will of its own that had nothing whatsoever to do with her good-girl upbringing or worries about the store. Finding out more about Olivia no longer seemed so important, not with the warmth of Matt seeping into every pore.

He flicked the key to the right, twisted the throttle. "Hang on tight."

That was an order she'd gladly follow. Katie wrapped her arms around Matt's waist, allowing herself to enjoy how easily she fit into him, how sensual it felt to mold her body to his. Her mother's voice echoed in the recesses of her brain, reminding her that good girls didn't fling themselves against men they barely knew. As a concession, Katie sat up a little straighter.

The engine erupted with life, the bike lurched forward. She was thrown against Matt, her chest pressed to the hard planes of his back, her thighs plastered along the length of his. Against the will of her more sensible parts, she melded to him.

And, my, did it feel good.

They roared down the street, moving as one with the bike, hugging the corners, slipping along the black river of road. Air rushed past Katie's face, fast and furious, as if she were caught in a summer storm.

It was terrifying. It was unnerving. It was also the most exhilarating thing she could ever remember doing, more exciting than the time she'd ridden the roller coaster at Cedar Point and had, for one split second, let go of the bar when the coaster began its wild descent from the peak.

This time, she had Matt to hold on to. Doing so helped her ignore the little voice of doubt inside her that told her she was just pretending, that she hadn't made any real changes in her life or herself yet. That the really scary stuff was yet to come.

Katie watched the road over his shoulder and inhaled the woodsy male scent of his cologne mingling with the wind as if he were part of the landscape that rushed past them in a blur of emerald and russet. Her hands splayed across his front, and under her fingertips, she could feel the rock-hardness of his chest.

She closed her eyes. Her thoughts veered into territory she'd never explored before. In her mind, she saw her own hands tugging up his T-shirt, roving over the ridges of muscles on his torso, dipping down to meet the waistband of his jeans, then roaming over his—

"You okay back there?"

She gulped in a breath. And promptly swallowed a bug. "Yeah, j-just f-fine," she stammered, trying not to gag or spit into Matt's hair. She prayed the insect that had just slid down her throat hadn't been a bee.

"Am I going too fast?"

It's my mind that's breaking the speed limit. "I'm fine."

"You sure? Do you want to stop or slow down?"

No. Yes. "No, I'm okay."

"We'll be there in a few minutes."

"Where is there?"

"You'll see. It's a surprise."

Katie tried to guess where he was taking her rather than think about the bug digesting in her stomach. They'd already passed the Corner Pocket and A Pair of Posies and were headed into the farm territory on the outskirts of town.

He slipped into a quiet, almost brooding silence the rest of the way. She considered broaching the subject of Olivia again but stopped herself. His reluctance to speak of Olivia had been as clear as a No Trespassing sign. He didn't want to talk about his past and she wouldn't force him. Not to mention, riding on a noisy motorcycle didn't exactly make conversation easy.

Matt turned onto a dirt road. He let out a sigh and the tension in his shoulders and back dissolved, as if whatever lay at the end of this road had been the antidote he needed for his mood.

There were no streetlights in this remote area and the early-morning half-darkness gathered in around them like a blanket. The wheels of the bike kicked up a cloud of dust, coating the windshield and blurring her vision. Matt slowed the bike, turned off the road and onto a grassy field.

Jane bumped and bucked over the rough landscape. "Having fun yet?" Matt turned and grinned at her.

"Do you take every woman you…you meet out to the middle of nowhere?"

"No, just you."

She refused to think about whether he was pretending to like her, whether he was still playing the charade, or how it would feel later when she went home. Instead, she studied his profile, illuminated by the spill of breaking sunlight overhead and forgot about the jostling motorcycle.

Matt was intent on driving, his gaze fixed on the wide

grassy tract ahead. He had a lean, chiseled face, full of strength and dependability. His jaw was set, firm.

Her gaze traveled down to his soft blue chambray shirt. The cuffs were rolled up, exposing defined wrists and wide, capable hands. His legs were clad in jeans that were well broken in, fitting him snugly and comfortably. She wondered what it would feel like to be those jeans, to skim over Matt's bare legs with the ease of familiarity.

"Here we are."

They were stopped in the middle of a huge field, backed by a cozy copse of trees. A few feet away stood a large barn that hadn't aged gracefully. Boards hung off it in various places, providing entry for the birds that flitted in and out. What had once been red paint on the exterior had faded to a rusty gray. She looked around for a farmhouse but saw only a half built foundation a hundred yards away, the two-by-fours sticking out of the cement base like a carpenter's version of Stonehenge.

"What is this place?"

"It used to be the Emery farm. Thirty years ago, there was a fire at the main house and it burned to the ground. Old Man Emery died in that fire, trying to save his house." Matt helped her off the bike, set it on its kickstand, then led her toward the barn. "The place was abandoned afterward. None of the Emery heirs wanted the farm, so it was on the market for a long time."

"I wonder why. It's a nice piece of land." She imagined the tall stalks of corn that must have grown here years ago, their silky tops bobbing in the breeze. She pictured cows grazing in the pasture to her left, kept in by the split-rail fence that had decayed and separated over the years.

"Some people think it's haunted since the owner died here." He creaked open the barn door and led her inside. He took a packet of matches out of his shirt pocket, struck one and bent to light a kerosene lantern sitting on a little table. "I just think it was an awful tragedy."

Light filled the room, warming the shadows and softening the gloom. Katie had expected the interior to be just as rundown and decrepit as the outside. But it wasn't. Someone had taken the time to sweep out the cobwebs, repair the floorboards and whisk out any rubble or hay that might have remained over the years.

In the center of the barn stood a small oval table, topped with a white tablecloth. There were two place settings of china, centered by a spray of yellow daisies in a vase. A pair of crystal goblets sat beside an ice bucket chilling a carafe of orange juice.

"When did you do all this?"

He came and stood before her, unhooking her helmet with nimble fingers that brushed the underside of her chin. "Before I picked you up this morning."

"You went to an awful lot of trouble."

"This place has always been kind of special to me. I wanted you to see it in the best possible light." He grinned. "I figured it would take the sting out of the work we'll be doing later."

He'd risen before the crack of dawn, hiked down here with silverware and glasses and set the whole thing up—complete with flowers—just for her. "It's beautiful."

"Thank you."

She wandered the room, stepping carefully on the old floorboards. "Why this one? Indiana has lots of old farmhouses."

"When I was younger, I used to come here when I wanted to get away from the house filled with antiques and crystal and things I couldn't touch." He drew her to the table, pulled out her chair and waited for her to sit. "I'd ride my bike out here and spend hours in this barn, pretending I was a farmer and this was my home."

"Is that what you wanted to be? A farmer?"

He chuckled. "When I was ten, farming looked mighty attractive. When I got older and realized how much work and money went into running a farm, I changed my mind. I'm happy doing construction work instead." He looked around the room and Katie saw a softening in his features, a vulnerability that slipped in when he wasn't guarding his emotions. "But I still loved the property. Something about the tragedy of it..." he paused, cleared his throat, went on, "When it went up for auction twelve years ago, I scraped together every penny I had and bought it. With my own money, not my father's."

From the way he said it, she knew that paying his own way was important to him. Once again, the Matt Webster of rumor and the real Matt were complete opposites.

Katie had already learned some hard lessons about image and reality. And how damaging that mirage could be to reality. The image of a happily engaged couple, so fragile another woman could easily steal the dream. The image of a successful businesswoman, hanging on to her store by a thread. The image of a woman who had moved on, yet was still desperately lonely because she was too scared to open up her heart and trust again. To fail again.

Katie pivoted in her seat, taking in the full view of the barn. "You own this property?"

"What's left of it."

"But why...? I mean, how come...?"

"Why does it look like this?" His hands gripped the back of his chair. "I started working on it when I bought it. Had great plans for the place. A two-story house over there," he pointed in the direction of the foundation, "a few animals here. Even a man-made pond out back."

"What happened?"

Matt swallowed hard. Katie's questions were opening doors he'd shut long ago. Doors that needed to be open, if he was ever going to get past that chapter in his life. What he needed to do, and what he was ready to do, however, were very different things.

"In one night, I lost everything that mattered to me." The words came out so softly Matt barely heard them himself. "And I no longer gave a damn about the house, or anything."

"Because you'd lost your baby?"

Katie couldn't have known how those words would affect him. He felt the familiar searing pain in his heart and had to take a deep breath before he could answer her. "Yes."

"I'm so sorry," she said, and he could hear the sympathy in her words. "It must have been awful for you."

"It was the worst thing that ever happened to me." His voice was hoarse. "I wasn't very good at dealing with it." *That* was an understatement.

"So you left town?"

"It seemed the best thing to do."

"But now you're back." She made a sweeping gesture of the room, as if sensing his need for a change of subject. "You have a great piece of land here. Are you finishing the house?"

He nodded. "Part of the reason I'm back is to finish what I started. This house is the first thing on my list."

"What's next?"

"That's as far as I've thought it out," he said. He wouldn't think about a wife or children. For now, for him, this was enough. He didn't have it in him to go through that kind of loss a second time. To have held hope in his arms and then to have it ripped away because of one stupid, foolish mistake.

A bird fluttered through the room, darting across their table before settling into a roost in the rafters. Katie didn't waver, didn't flinch. She watched him, her gaze open, trusting.

He knew she wasn't the kind of woman who would be in and out of his life after a night or two. He didn't know what he'd been thinking when he'd come up with this crazy plan to spend more time with her, here and at the wedding. Well, hell, he did know. He'd been thinking of himself, of the way that kiss had seared his soul, of being close to this woman who seemed to have a bead on the bull's-eye of his heart.

One thing was certain, he hadn't been thinking of her. She wasn't a woman to trifle with, one he could use and throw away. She had a lot more at stake than he. All he'd selfishly wanted was an excuse to spend a few more hours with the woman who'd invaded his every waking thought. He hadn't been looking for anything more than that. But he could see, from the reflection in her gaze, she'd already begun caring about what happened to him.

The thought alternately flattered and terrified him.

"Katie, this is probably way too soon," he began, "but I should be up front with you, so we're clear from the start." He swallowed. "There's not going to be anything beyond our deal. I'm not getting involved in a serious relationship and I'm certainly not getting married again. Hell, I'm not even the kind of guy who should be married."

"Why?"

"Because I'm lousy at commitment."

"You're committed to this house," she said, catching him in the lie. "What makes you think you're no good for marriage?"

"Do you always ask this many questions?"

"Do you always evade answering them?"

"Touché." He smiled, forcing the dark mood that had persistently tried to invade the day from settling inside him. He pushed thoughts of the past away and focused his attention on the very appealing present.

He was alone with a beautiful, intriguing woman. He'd be a fool to spend that time dwelling on what could not be undone. Instead, he'd focus on the things he could undo. Like the buttons on the kitten-soft sweater Katie wore.

Whoa, Romeo. What were you just saying about nothing beyond the deal?

"I forgot our breakfast in the bike's cooler." He left the barn before his fingers started doing, or rather undoing, the things his mind was fantasizing about.

Katie settled against her chair and considered what Matt had just told her. She'd heard the rumors about his child's death and about his marriage, but obviously, those hadn't begun to tell the truth. People had painted Matt as an unfeeling wealthy cad who had abandoned his wife for the open road.

She knew now, from watching the pain that had washed across his face and strained his voice, those rumors were far from the truth. Matt had been deeply affected.

But he wasn't ready for anything beyond a few dates and a few nights in bed. He might never be ready. The last thing Katie wanted right now was to get involved with another Steve. At twenty-four, she'd stopped taking relationships halfway. There was no point in spending weeks, months, even years, with someone who wasn't investing all he had. She was tired of being alone. Of wondering what life might hold if she could just get past the rut she'd buried herself in. Of watching Sarah and Jack build a future together, with a home, children.

Meeting Matt had given her a taste of courage to try the things she'd been missing for the past year—no, all her life.

He'd sparked a fire that had never been anything more than day-old embers with Steve. She was exploring things she'd never considered before, that she'd only read about in books and thought had just been the fiction of a writer's overactive mind.

But along with all those new feelings were the seeds of questions about herself. She'd said she wanted a change, a more adventurous approach to living. Yet every step she took in that direction scared her as much as it excited her. Matt had lived the opposite—taking off for parts unknown when he was young. Thumbing his nose at the town, at everyone who disagreed with him. She envied him for that.

What had she been so afraid of all these years? What had stopped her from living a life full of more than reruns and organized cans in the cabinet?

Somewhere along the path of her life, Katie Dole had decided not to take chances. Until Matt came along.

But right now, he was a risk of epic proportions. She was starting to like him. Too much. The best thing to do was leave, to walk away before her heart became too entangled.

She was halfway out of her chair when Matt re-entered the barn, framed by the rising sun like a portrait of a cowboy hero, and she knew she couldn't leave. Not yet. If she did, she'd always wonder *what if.*

Besides, she'd made a deal. All she had to do was help him today and then she could go. But as her heart hammered at his approach, she knew there was far more involved for her than that.

And, he'd brought breakfast—a breakfast that came in bags decorated with golden arches. She laughed. "My, my, you do go all out for a girl, don't you?"

"Egg and cheese sandwiches, with extra bacon—the breakfast of champions."

"Mmm, they smell great," she murmured, selecting one.

"Only the best for you, Katie Dole."

"I've heard that line before," she said wryly. "And that best left me standing at the altar."

"He didn't know what he was leaving behind."

"He knew what he was leaving with," she muttered. "Or rather, who."

"You deserve better than him."

She held his gaze. What *did* Matt want? He danced around talk of a relationship like a bee unsure whether the flower was a Venus flytrap or a lily. "Are you saying you would be a better choice than Steve?"

"How about some orange juice?" He grabbed the carafe by the neck and yanked it out of the bucket. A fine spray of water scattered over them and the table.

"There you go again, changing the subject." Katie began eating her sandwich. "You're awfully good at that."

"I'm good at a lot of things."

A soft sigh that was almost a purr escaped her. "That, I know. Firsthand."

She was beautiful in the amber light of the lantern, beautiful and tempting and desirable. Soft shadows outlined her face, tracing along her body, and he found himself wishing there was a bed in the barn so he could explore those curves the way they deserved to be explored.

But he'd decided when he went out to the motorcycle for breakfast that he wasn't going to go there. A girl like Katie ought to have a promise of forever and a man who would keep it. And then, he suspected, the floodgates of passion— of the true Katie, who had probably been kept in check all her life—would open to the man she loved. A fleeting image of her doing just that rippled through his mind.

Pour the juice; don't spill it on the table. His hand was

unsteady and a puddle of orange had formed around the base of the glass. That's what he got for letting his thoughts run to peeling off her clothes and tasting the sweet, warm skin underneath.

Every time he saw her, or his mind even wandered to thinking about her, red-hot fire rushed through his groin. He needed a dousing with ice water just to concentrate on the simplest tasks and to stop him from whisking her off to bed tonight. And tomorrow night. And the next night.

Until those nights began to pile up into something more, something that would tempt him to hang around for years— forever. For Matt, that was his cue to leave.

He might not be a perfect man, but he was enough of one to know those boundaries were ones he shouldn't cross. Not with a woman like her. But, damn, he wanted to cross them all anyway.

She leaned her chin on her hand. "Tell me. What exactly does our 'deal' entail?"

He grinned. "The curiosity is eating you up, isn't it?"

"Well…yeah."

"You know I own a construction company?"

"Yes, I heard you tell Miss Marchand."

"Well, my guys are busy finishing up a big job back in Pennsylvania. They won't be here for another week. I'm anxious to get out of my parents' house and into my own. But it's a little hard to build a house by yourself."

"Why not hire a local crew?"

"Because it's much more fun to ask you to help me." When he'd come up with the idea in the bar, it had seemed perfect. An excuse, he knew, to see her again. To be a good guy for once and help her show Steve Spencer she was an incredible woman. It was just a deal, he told himself. A favor. For a friend. *Yeah, right.*

"Matt, in case you haven't noticed, I'm a pint-sized

weakling." She flexed her arm muscle as proof. "I'm not sure I even know how to hold a hammer."

"Right now, I have some demolition work to do. Nothing big, nothing I need a whole crew for. The real work will start when the rest of the supplies are delivered. The studs I put up eleven years ago are warped and need to be replaced. You don't have to do much more than hold on while I rip out the old stud and put up a new one. Besides, I could use the company."

"That's all you want?"

No, I also want a bed and you in it. Naked. With me. "Yep, that's it."

"And in exchange, you'll go to Steve and Barbara's wedding with me on Saturday?"

He nodded. "And pretend to be your fiancé so that you can show 'Stevie' that you've moved on. In a big way." He grinned.

"But I don't understand why you'd pretend to be engaged to me. From what you just said, that's the kind of commitment you won't get within ten feet of."

Because it gives me an excuse to keep seeing you, even though I know I shouldn't. He couldn't say that, so he told another lie, one as flimsy as the boards holding the barn together, because the truth—his internal war between wanting to get close to her and wanting to roar out of town on Jane—was impossible to voice.

"Because it'll be fun to turn this town on its ear again. You're looking to ruin your reputation. I'm looking to repair mine. Being with what my mother would call a 'nice girl,'" he grinned a wicked smile, taking pleasure in the flush that ran down her neck, "would certainly change my image."

"Well, I'm not looking to ruin my reputation, just smudge it a bit." She laughed. "I've been Conventional Katie way too long."

"That's a heck of a nickname." He considered her. "Somehow, it doesn't seem to fit you."

"You met me after I changed my life motto."

"And what is your motto now?"

"To live life to the fullest, before it passes me by," she said with a nod, as if she'd just reminded herself, too.

"That's a hell of a good motto, Katie Dole," he said, and meant it. He had seen the years slip by in lonely nights spent in bars, trying to drown out the memories that only good beer and later, when he was sober, hard work seemed to erase. He was thirty, and a third of his life had already been spent in atonement.

"Let's put it to work and get started on that house." He tossed his napkin on the table and got to his feet. He was suddenly anxious to tear down those old walls and get the new lumber into place. For his new life.

Chapter Six

With a hammer in her hand and sawdust in her hair, Katie's new life was decidedly hard work. The old timbers were heavy, the new ones even more so. As the sun rose and warmed the sky, working on Matt's house became more and more of a workout. Her arms ached, her back twinged with pain and she could feel the beginning of a sunburn on her nose.

But she didn't mind. Every minute that passed steamed with a growing attraction between her and Matt, one she was sure she wasn't imagining. Even though he'd professed not to want a relationship, Katie found herself fantasizing about just that, and about a lot more than the kiss they'd shared in the store.

"Ouch!" She jumped back, away from the two-by-four that had stabbed her, leaving an angry red mark on her finger. For an innocent-looking piece of wood, it had one heck of a mean streak. That's what she got for being distracted by thoughts of Matt.

"Here, let me see that." He took her hand in his. All day,

there'd been these little touches, some accidental, some on purpose. It was as if working together in the quiet stillness had brought them closer.

Well, the splinters had helped, too.

Tenderly, Matt lifted her finger to the light and examined the tiny shaft of wood protruding from her thumb. "That's a bad one. But, not as bad as your last one."

"Or the one before that."

"Or the one just before that." He grinned. With a set of tweezers he'd told her he kept in his toolbox, Matt carefully extracted the splinter, just as he had the other three. When he was done, he lifted her hand to his lips and placed a soft kiss on the red mark, just as he had done earlier. And Katie's heart skipped a beat at the tenderness of the gesture, just as it had three times before.

But this time, Matt didn't let go of her hand and turn back to his work. Electricity hummed between them, simmering like the sun that blazed above them. "Maybe this wasn't such a good idea."

"What?"

"Having you work on the house with me. You're getting injured," he kissed her palm and the heat seared her skin, "every five seconds."

"It's okay."

"No, it's not. I don't like seeing you get hurt."

"They're just splinters. I get thorns in my fingers all the time from the roses at the shop. I can handle a splinter."

"I'm sure you can," he said. "I think, though, that you deserve a little TLC for all your efforts." He dipped his head towards hers, his mouth hovering over her lips. Waiting, wanting. Desire curled between them, a rope growing tauter by the second. "Tender." Matt took a breath. "Loving." Released it. "Care."

She wanted him. His lips on hers again, his touch warm

against her skin. Taking a tremendous, daring chance, Katie stretched forward just enough for her lips to brush Matt's.

When she did, he let out a moan that sounded like her name and then kissed her. The moment his mouth met hers, hot fire raced through her, ten times stronger than at the grocery store. She wrapped her arms around his chest and stood on tiptoe to have more of him.

His lips claimed hers with a hunger that matched hers. His hands roamed along her back, dancing a tune all along her spine. She could feel his heart beating, merging with the rhythm of her own. Blood rushed through her veins, tingled against her nerves. She opened her mouth to his, amazed that something so simple as a kiss could feel so stupendously wonderful.

"Katie, Katie, Katie," he murmured against her mouth. "I've been trying all day not to do that."

"I can't think of a good reason why we shouldn't." And she couldn't, not now. All those justifications she'd had earlier today seemed miles away. "Can you?"

"Hell, no." He hauled her against him. Instinct pressed her pelvis to his, wanting, needing, seeking what she'd never had before. She trailed her hands down his back—

"I see you've found a way to spend your days."

A man's voice sliced through the air with razor sharpness. Katie jerked out of Matt's arms and turned, silently cursing the intruder's timing.

A tall man, the kind who commanded attention and deference just in the way he held himself, zeroed in on Katie like a hawk spotting a mouse scurrying across the ground. His dark-gray suit, perfectly tailored and precisely fitted, screamed *expensive* and *top-notch designer*. Even coated with a fine layer of dust, Katie suspected his shoes didn't come from this side of the Atlantic.

"Hello, Father," said Matt. "What a surprise."

So this was Edward Webster. He looked every bit as daunting as his reputation.

"Katie, this is my father, Edward," Matt said, taking her hand in his. "Father, this is Katie Dole, my…"

Girlfriend. Pretend fiancée. Maybe the love of my life. Katie supplied a number of mental tags but Matt obviously wasn't telepathic.

"…friend," he finished. "Close friend."

"I could see that," Edward replied dryly. "All the way from the road." He cleared his throat. "I came by to see what you were doing. Your mother said you were rebuilding this house. I wondered why."

"I need a place to live."

"Why this house?"

"Because I already happen to own it."

Edward picked his way slowly around the rooms-to-be, peering at the new wood Matt had erected. He grabbed one of the posts and gave it a firm shake, testing it for stability, Katie supposed. "And you're going to do this all by yourself?"

"I have Katie to help me."

Edward's gaze told her exactly what he thought about her abilities to construct a house. "And?"

"And my crew will be here in a week. They're finishing up the last two houses in a development I bought last year."

Edward cocked his head. "You bought? Your crew?"

"My business has done very well, Father."

"I wasn't aware of that."

"You never asked."

"I hadn't expected…" Edward's voice trailed off.

"That I'd do anything more than drink and raise Cain?"

"Well…"

Katie could see the two men were at an impasse, both stiff and unyielding in their posture, and most likely in their minds as well. She hefted one of the newly delivered two-by-fours from the pile in the corner and began dragging it over to an empty spot on the sill plate.

"Katie, what are you doing?"

"You'll never get your house built standing around talking all day." She turned to Matt's father and offered him a friendly smile. "Mr. Webster, would you mind toenailing this in while I hold it?" After two hours working with Matt, she already had the construction jargon down pat. Another hour and she'd be sporting a cowhide tool belt and holding nails with her teeth. "Did you bring a hammer?"

Edward's eyebrows lifted. "Hammer?"

"If you're here, you might as well help." Katie bent down and grabbed her own hammer. "Here, use mine. There's a pile of nails by your foot. Now, I'll hold this and if you wouldn't mind, could you nail two of those long ones in at an angle to the bottom?" Edward gaped at her as she talked in a steady stream of words that left no room for refusal.

He hesitated. She'd shocked the patriarch of the Webster family. *Now that's something the old Katie never would have done. Nor would she have done that kiss earlier.*

Just when she thought Edward Webster would either turn into a statue or walk away, he bent down in his designer suit and Italian shoes and drove two nails home, without wasting a stroke or denting the wood. That was a lot better than she'd done all day. Virtually every piece of wood in this place bore a dimpled circle from where Katie had completely missed the nail.

"You shouldn't be doing that." Matt hurried over and took the hammer from him. He put a hand under Edward's elbow and supported him as he got to his feet. "I'm sure your doctor's orders don't include building a house."

Matt turned to Katie. "My father had a heart attack three

weeks ago. He's supposed to stay home and *rest*." He eyed Edward.

"Oh, God, I'm really sorry. I didn't know—"

"It's been a long time since I did that," Edward cut in, rubbing his chin thoughtfully. "Must be twenty years since I picked up a hammer."

"And if Mom hears about this, it will be twenty years before you do it again." Matt tucked Katie's hammer into his tool belt.

"I'd forgotten what it's like to build something with my own two hands." Edward gripped the two-by-four and smiled, lost in a reverie. "You know, I built the first house your mother and I lived in."

Matt's jaw dropped. "You did?"

Edward's voice dipped to a lower pitch, the memories drifting from him in tendrils. "It was a tiny thing, just a two-bedroom ranch on a slab. I worked on it every weekend and after work. Took me the better part of a year, even with your grandfather and Uncle Charlie helping."

"You did?" Matt repeated.

A soft smile Matt hadn't seen in years lingered on his father's face, smoothing away decades. The father he knew never reminisced about the past or about building houses. But here Edward was, doing exactly that. His animosity toward his son had also temporarily disappeared, replaced by a man Matt actually felt he could talk to. That had to be the biggest shock of all.

"After that, you were born and I bought Webster Enterprises," Edward continued. "I never had time to build anything again." He patted the stud. His gaze sharpened and he gave one last look at the post before dusting off his hands and turning away. "I guess it's like riding a bike. You never really forget."

"I didn't know that about you." Matt leaned against the framework.

"You never asked."

"I didn't think…" Matt began, realizing then that they were repeating their first conversation, but with the roles reversed. "You surprised me, Father."

"Well," Edward cleared his throat. "I better get back before your mother starts to worry. I just wanted to see what you were doing."

Matt joined his father, walking slowly with him away from the house and down the dirt driveway to the gleaming silver Mercedes. As they approached the car and distanced themselves from common ground, the détente between them ebbed away.

Matt opened the door and held it while Edward lowered himself to the leather seat. "You're probably not supposed to be driving either, right?"

Edward scowled and waved his hand in dismissal of medical science. "The doctors want me tied to that house for weeks. A man can't live like that. I'm not planning on running the Boston Marathon. I just wanted some fresh air."

"And to check up on me."

He planted his hands on either side of the steering wheel and nodded. "Yes."

"Father, I'm thirty years old. I'm too old to run around town tipping cows and busting mailboxes."

"That doesn't stop me from being your father, Matthew." He slid the key into the ignition and started the car. "I'll see you at the house."

"When it's okay with your doctor…" Matt hesitated before finishing a sentence he'd never started before.

Edward looked up, his hand on the gearshift. "Yes?"

"…and if you want to, you're welcome to help with the house."

His father blinked twice, then nodded. "I'd like that, Matthew." His voice sounded hoarse with emotion. Impossible. Edward Webster had no soft side. He cleared his throat and shook his head. "Damned heart medications have me acting like a loon." He fingered the keys on the ring. "Forgot the house key again. I hope your mother hasn't left for her committee meeting yet."

Matt fished his house key out of his pocket and held it out. Edward's hand trembled when he took the metal piece, but then he barked a goodbye and put the car in gear.

Katie came up and laid a hand on his shoulder. "That was a nice surprise—your father stopping by."

Her touch stirred something in him, something both warm and coolly soothing.

"It was nice. He's not the same man he used to be."

"Yesterday, you said the same thing about yourself."

He chuckled. "You're awfully wise for someone so beautiful."

She turned a pretty shade of red, like apples with their first blush of color. Katie was too young for him, too innocent, too…too perfect. He'd tried damned hard to resist her, but it wasn't working. All day, he'd purposely avoided kissing her, working as hard at keeping their "deal" platonic as he had at tearing down the old framing on the house. So far, he'd only been successful with the lumber. If staying away from Katie were a graded assignment, he'd have a big fat F.

"Well," she said, "you're running out of time for help. I have to get back to the store in a little while."

"Then let's get back to work." But instead of loping up the hill to the house, Matt lowered his mouth to Katie's and captured her again.

Riding back to her apartment on Jane was not as much fun as it had been this morning. Once Matt dropped her off, their day would end and she'd have to go to work. For the first time, Katie wanted to play hooky from A Pair of Posies.

She wanted to stay with Matt. Yet, even as she inched forward on the bike, plastering her torso to his back, she was telling herself that she shouldn't get any closer to this man, physically or otherwise.

He'd already made it clear he was a no-commitment guy. She'd fallen for one of those before and didn't want to repeat that mistake. Yet every minute with Matt wrapped her tighter in an emotional cocoon that demanded a price she didn't have the heart to pay.

It was useless to resist—her heart had stopped listening to her mind ever since he'd kissed her.

Much too soon, her apartment came into view. Matt pulled up to the curb and cut the ignition. With a sigh, Katie slid off the bike and removed her helmet. She glanced up at the yellow-and-white Victorian building that housed her apartment. She should be in there, getting ready for work. But suddenly, entering that empty apartment seemed to be the saddest thing she could do.

"Thanks for your help." Matt took her helmet and clipped it to the back. "It's nearly two. You have to get to work, and…" his hand grazed her cheek. "And if I stay, I might forget we're only pretending at this."

"Are we?"

"Hmm…I'm not so sure." He grinned. "Let's try it one more time and see." He brushed his lips over hers. Again. And again.

The man was a magician. His kisses released feelings she hadn't even known she had, like doves from under his sleeve. His tongue swept the recesses of her mouth, teasing hers back, urging her to do the same. She pressed her chest to his, nearly clawing at his back to get closer, taste more, have more. More of what, she couldn't say.

"You're going to be late," he murmured. "Very late."

Before she could think twice, Katie blurted out, "Will you walk me to my door?" And then, because she didn't want it to seem that she was inviting him into her bed— even she wasn't sure she wasn't—she added, "Sweet Pea usually gets his afternoon walk around now and I'm afraid he might mistake me for lunch."

Matt chuckled. "He did find you appetizing this morning."

"Must be my eau de steak."

"Something like that," Matt murmured, leaning down and starting again, this time with her neck. "Mmm…you are delicious. Done to perfection."

She heard the squeals of playing children from the house down the street. "I think we should get inside before the neighbors see us."

"What's the worst that could happen? Everyone thinks we're crazy about each other?" He grinned. "Isn't that the goal? To make people believe we're engaged?"

"Yes, it is." But Katie's heart was heavy. She no longer wanted to pretend, didn't want his kisses to be part of a "deal." She wanted Matt for real. And just like Steve, he wasn't interested in anything permanent. "I'm sure the neighbors get the point."

"Okay, I'll be on my best behavior then."

Katie started up the steps of the house, vacillating about hoping Matt followed. Earlier, she'd decided not to get involved with him. But after spending the day with him, working side by side and trading jokes along with nails, she'd started to feel differently. The quiet conversations they'd had and the tender way he'd treated her had touched her as had no other man she'd known. Who else would take such time and care with a splinter? Who else would have made sure she took a break and had a drink every hour? What other man had ever kissed her as if she were a precious gift, someone he wanted to please, not someone who was there to please him?

She'd never known a man like Matt. Now she was inviting him in, delaying his departure. Feeling hope when he'd said the neighbors might interpret their kiss as them being "crazy about each other." Was there a possibility that he was thinking about something more? Or was she grasping at imaginary straws?

"Tell me about your store," Matt said as they entered the building and started up the two flights leading to her apartment.

"Well, Sarah and I always dreamed of having our own shop," Katie said, venturing onto the safer ground of talking about the store instead of asking the questions burning inside her. "We saved our money, went to college for business and design. We found the perfect location last April. We figured it would take two more years to save enough for all the supplies we'd need to open. But when Steve dumped me, I used my half of the honeymoon money to finance the startup.

"In the end," she said as they reached the final step and walked down the hall toward her apartment, "breaking up with Steve was the best thing that ever happened to me."

"I agree. It left you free for me," Matt murmured.

She wheeled around. "And what does that mean? Are we seeing each other? Are we fulfilling a deal?" She swallowed. "Or is there more to it than that for you?"

Matt could see the apprehension in her gaze. She'd asked a question, but wasn't sure of the answer. Hell, neither was he.

Were they seeing each other, in the classic meaning of

the term? They were talking, doing the dance of sexual innuendo and flirting glances that eventually led to the bedroom. It was a dance he knew the steps to by heart, one that
didn't require much more of a commitment than an evening
between the sheets.

Katie, however, wasn't a woman who made temporary
commitments. And even if she did agree to a night in his
bed, Katie would expect—no, need—more. And as much as
he was tempted to try that path again, he couldn't. The one
time he had...the consequences had been devastating.
Nearly destroying him.

He wasn't strong enough to go through that hell again,
even for her, a woman who had intrigued him more than
anyone he'd ever met in his life. He was fine with today,
with fulfilling the deal they'd made, but after that—

She was waiting for his answer.

"We're together now," he replied.

"And tomorrow? Where will you be then?"

He skimmed his thumbs over her fingers. Her skin was
soft, velvety smooth. He imagined how the rest of her would
feel, pictured her sliding along his body and slipping onto
him, smoothly, easily, achingly perfectly.

"Still with you, eating breakfast in our pajamas," he answered, releasing the words throbbing in his mind.

"I can't, Matt. I'm not...I don't give my heart easily.
Call me old-fashioned." Her smile was weak. Yet, in her
eyes, the spark of desire lingered. Push. Pull. Even he didn't
know what he wanted anymore.

"Oh, Katie. What am I going to do with you?" He pulled
her closer, dipping to kiss the hollow of her neck.

She sighed, a wonderful throaty sound that echoed against
his lips. "I don't know."

"I can't change your mind?" He left a trail of kisses
along her chin and up to the corner of her mouth. He wanted

her to say yes, to give in. He wanted in and out of her life without any damage to himself.

"No." The word was exhaled on a shaky breath.

Say yes. Be with me. He claimed her mouth with his, intending to tease her into agreement. But when their lips met, Katie moaned and leaned into him. "Matt."

An explosion of desire rocked him. His hands tangled in her hair, lifting the silky chestnut tresses and letting them slip through his fingers like a waterfall. Her breasts crushed against his chest, her pelvis tilting to his. The only thing stopping them from more was their clothing.

He slipped a hand between them and snuck it under the front of her shirt, forgetting they were standing in her hallway and hadn't even made it into her apartment yet. He cupped her breast through the lace of her bra with his palm, teased the nub of her nipple with his fingers. A perfect fit. Everything about her was perfect, as if she'd been created just for him.

"Matt…Matt," she repeated, more firmly.

"Mmm?"

She pulled back and grabbed his hand. "I think…" she took a breath. "I think we should stop. This isn't…it can't end up the way you want it to."

Desire still pulsed through his veins and from the flush on Katie's face, he knew she shared that feeling. But the lady had said no and she'd meant it. And she was right.

He backed away, willing his body to stop responding to her nearness. His arousal, hemmed in by his jeans, was a painful reminder of how long it would take for the effect she was having on him to wear off. "I'm not very good at keeping my promise of being on my best behavior, am I?"

"No, you're not." Her smile was forgiving. "It isn't because I don't want you…because…I do. More than you know." She took in a deep breath. "We want different things, Matt. I'm not a halfway kind of girl. For me, being with you halfway won't be enough. As much as I would like to continue this," she pressed a finger to his lips and the flame of desire roared to life again, "I can't. I'm sorry."

Katie Dole wanted it all. The passion, the romance and down the road, words that would bind them together for more than a few nights. For a lifetime. Those were words that no longer existed in his vocabulary. They hadn't been there in a long, long time.

"I don't think I can give you what you're asking for." The words caught in his throat.

"And that's the problem." She sighed. "I don't want a commitment today. I only want the door to be open. Can you understand that?"

"Yes." A long time ago, he'd wanted to walk that same path. But now… "I'm no longer the kind of guy who gets married, settles down in a suburb and has two-point-five kids and a dog. I tried that, it didn't work."

"I'm not saying I want to get married immediately or anything like that. Lord knows I'm still trying to sort out the mess from last year. It's just that I'm not the kind of woman who can give everything…" She closed her eyes briefly and shook her head. "…and be left with nothing. After today, it's not just pretending for me." Her voice cracked. "Not anymore."

It wasn't for him either. But he didn't say that. Another door he kept shut.

"It was never my intention to mislead you or to let today get out of hand. But it did." He stroked his hand along her cheek. "We could have a lot of fun together over the next few weeks, Katie. Would that be so awful?"

"If I were a different girl, maybe not." She clasped his hand. "But I'm not looking for a one-night stand. I'm not the kind of woman who takes sex, or love for that matter, lightly. I've already been through that game with a guy who wouldn't stick around and I can't do it again." She let go and turned to slip her key into the lock. "I had a nice time today, Matt. A really nice time. But I don't think I can do this. I tried to, but…I can't. I'm sorry."

"Katie, wait, don't go." He touched her arm. With a sigh of regret, she brushed his hand away and stepped back.

"You and I want different things, Matt. Better to find that out now than three weeks or three years from now. Our deal is off. I wish you well."

She opened the door and walked into her apartment, shutting the door before he could enter. He heard her slide the deadbolt into place, locking him out and herself in.

Chapter Seven

It was Friday, six days since she'd helped Matt at his house. Every single one had passed without a phone call, without even a sight of him, though she'd heard his name mentioned a thousand times. Speculations and rumors were flying fast and furious, with people stopping by the store to offer congratulations while trying to unearth more gossip about the Devil of Mercy's alliance with Conventional Katie.

Her plan had worked—Katie was no longer the pitied, jilted bride; she was hovering on the brink of wantonness. She should have been happy.

But she was utterly miserable.

Did she think she could change a man with one conversation? Over a couple of egg sandwiches? To be honest, yes, she'd half hoped Matt would see a relationship wasn't some kind of communicable disease.

Obviously, that hadn't been the case. Matthew Webster wanted to slip in and out of her life as quickly and as unpredictably as a summer thunderstorm. And what a storm

he would be, she thought, recalling his touch, the taste of
his lips.

She put a halt to thoughts of Matt. The *last* thing she
needed was another guy who wanted a fling—and nothing
more. Once before, she'd fallen in love with a man who
hadn't been marriage—or any other kind of permanence—
material and had ended up hurt. And alone. How ironic that
she'd managed to make that mistake twice in a little over a
year.

"Katie? Anyone home?"

"Huh?" Katie jerked upright. "I'm sorry, Sarah, I didn't
hear you."

"I was saying I still can't believe what a week it's been!
Between people stopping by the store, to 'casually' mention
that they heard about your pretend 'engagement,' to the way
business picked up, I feel like we've been sitting on a star
or something. Olivia Maguire's orders alone will make up
the shortfall on the rent." Sarah waddled out from behind
the counter, carrying a dish garden she had adorned with a
sage-colored ribbon. She placed the ceramic container of
plants beside several others that Katie was arranging in a
display.

"You are the talk of Mercy," Sarah continued. "That
story about you kissing Matt in Sav-a-Lot has grown to epic
proportions, with some saying you tackled him to the floor."

"I did not!"

"I know that, but gossip in this town always gets out of
hand." Sarah trimmed a few dead leaves from a potted
plant. "Miss Tanner is the only one who isn't thrilled. She
came in here with that moose of hers and told me what a
rotten no-good man you've hitched yourself to." She
grinned. "I told her I've met Matt and thought he was
sweet."

"Sweet? I don't think we're talking about the same

man." Katie laid a sheet of crimson fabric over an old worn table. She stuffed some boxes under the fabric to provide varied height stands for the arrangements. "Well, if nothing else, I'm glad this deal with Matt has increased sales, because right now, I'm engaged to the invisible man."

"He'll be back."

"No, I don't think so." The dish garden completed, Katie turned to work on a half finished silk arrangement on the counter. "Matt made it clear he's not interested in anything real."

"Try again, Katie." Sarah laid a hand over hers. "This one looks like a keeper."

"Looks can be deceiving." Katie jabbed a bunch of faux baby's breath into the arrangement. She added several fern fronds to the back and sides, turning the container and tucking greenery in here and there.

"You'll never know unless you go out with him again."

"I don't think that's going to happen," she replied. "The wedding is tomorrow night and since I told him the deal is off, it looks like I'm going stag or not at all."

"I think you should invite him anyway. Drag him off to the wedding like a cavewoman with a prize mastodon."

Katie chuckled, then sobered. "Why? I'll just end up hurt and alone after the rice hits the ground."

"Katie, Katie, Katie. Have I taught you nothing?" Sarah grabbed Katie's shoulders. "If you're with him and he's pretending to love you, it could be a nice taste of the real thing. He might like it so much, he falls in love…for real."

"I've thought of that."

"And?"

"It could just as easily be me who does the falling in love, not him."

"You're already halfway there, aren't you?"

Katie focused her attention on the arrangement rather than

on the truth in Sarah's question. She shouldn't have brought up his name. Every time she talked about Matt, she felt a sharp pang. He'd opened a different side of her self, encouraged her to taste more of what life offered. And at the same time, he'd treated her with a reverence and a tenderness she'd never known before. He was a contradiction in what he said and what he did and she sensed he hoped for more for himself, but didn't know how to get it.

Ever since that first kiss and the way he'd played along with her charade, she'd hoped he'd be interested in more than a fling. But he hadn't been and that fact was driving itself home, straight through her heart.

"Even if he did fall in love," Katie said, "which I doubt he would, he's told me he's not looking for anything permanent."

"What guy is? Katie," she said in a solemn, confidential voice, "it's our job as women to teach men what a great thing monogamy really is."

"Apparently I'm not a very good teacher," Katie scoffed. "Look at Steve. If anything, I made him more of a womanizer."

"Steve is a walking advertisement for neutering."

Katie laughed. Imagining Steve on an SPCA poster, encouraging women to get their straying mates neutered, was the funniest thing she'd thought of all day. "You never did like Steve much, did you?"

"I always thought you could do better, Katie. I know you always hoped he'd change, but I don't think Steve was ready to grow up. I knew you wouldn't listen to me. You had to figure that out on your own." Sarah handed Katie a carnation. "Anyway, let's get back to Mr. Right—"

The door jangled and Olivia Maguire breezed in. Today, she was dressed in head-to-toe crimson, the perfect contrast for her pale blond hair and ivory features. If Katie didn't know better, she'd swear Olivia had just come from a fashion shoot at Versace.

"Those arrangements were a hit with my customers," Olivia said by way of introduction. "I'd like to start working with you on future projects."

"That would be great," Sarah said. Katie had to force herself not to clap or dance with joy. The increased business had great potential for helping them out of their financial slump.

"I work with a number of clients in town," Olivia began. "And I just got the contract to oversee the rest of the renovations at the Lawford Country Club. Seems the first designer didn't get it right." She whisked a stray hair back into place in a single, graceful movement. "There's plenty of work for your shop through my company. Plenty."

"We'd be happy to work with—"

"Lots of contacts with some of the affluent people in the area," Olivia interrupted before Sarah could finish. "Exactly what your shop needs, from what I've heard."

"It would be nice, yes," Katie said. *Nice* was an understatement.

"Great. Maybe a partnership could be beneficial to both of us." Olivia extracted a pile of business cards from her purse. "You spread the word about my business, and I'll do the same for you."

"I'd be happy to do that." Katie took the cards and placed them in a visible spot by the cash register. She handed a few of the shop's cards to Olivia. When she did, she thought she saw a flicker of distrust in Olivia's eyes, but it disappeared as quickly as it came.

"Thank you." Olivia tucked them into her purse, then crossed to the display of dish gardens. "I'd like to order two of these, in that stoneware dish you have there. They'd be great on the lobby tables." She tapped a finger on her chin, back in business mode. "I also have a client who is looking for something to jazz up her kitchen. Can you design one with a miniature herb garden? Kind of country chic?"

"Certainly," Sarah said. "We have one over here that's growing really well." She led Olivia to another display.

Within a few minutes, Olivia had settled on her order. Before she left, she stopped by Katie. "I'm happy we'll be working together. Your business is the perfect complement to mine." Her gaze narrowed. "I'm glad to see it's as important to you as mine is to me."

What did that mean? Had Olivia heard Katie and Matt were dating? Was she angry? Before Katie could ask, Olivia was gone, leaving a trail of expensive perfume in her wake.

"Come on, let's celebrate. You look like you could use a pick-me-up." Sarah waved Katie over to the door in the back that led to their combination lunchroom and storage area. "Besides, I have a surprise for you." With a flourish, Sarah flung open the door. "Ta da! Our latest money-maker."

Hanging on the coat rack was a clown suit so loud and garish, it would have embarrassed Ronald McDonald. The wig, a rainbow of fuzzy hair sticking up and out, looked as if it had been struck by lightning. The clown outfit was purple, decorated with orange and green spots and enormous matching pompoms running down the center. Two-foot-long black-and-purple shoes lay beside the suit, completing the ensemble.

"Oh no, not me." Katie backed away from the glaring costume. "It was bad enough being a banana. I'm not running around town dressed like Bozo."

"The only people who will see you are under the age of ten. Besides, once you get the makeup on, no one will know it's you."

"There's makeup, too? As in big red lips and U-brows?" Katie shook her head. "How is this going to help us make money? If anything, I'll scare the customers away."

"It's for birthday parties. I got some money from my father for my birthday and well...put it toward the store." She flushed a little, anticipating Katie's protests before she finished. "Don't say it. I want the store to succeed, too. The suit was marked down and was too good a deal to pass up. I ordered a small helium tank so we can start delivering balloons." She put up a hand when Katie started to sputter a response. "You don't have to perform, just show up, twist together a couple of balloon animals and wave goodbye to the kiddies. An easy twenty-five bucks. Besides, our competition doesn't do anything like that. We'd be the only clowns in town." Sarah grinned and tugged the outfit off the hanger, handing the wig to Katie.

"Here, see if it fits. There was another one at the costume shop but it looked like it might be too big for you."

Katie looked at the Paul Bunyan-size shoes and the tent of a clown suit. "Oh yeah, this is just my size. What is this? A three...hundred?"

Sarah laughed. She slipped her hands under the wig, stretching it to fit Katie's skull. "Come on, be a sport."

"No one I know better see me in this getup," Katie told her as she stepped into the flowing purple jumper, "or my reputation as a serious businesswoman is shot."

"That went out the window the day you agreed to stand on a street corner in a banana suit." Sarah came around to Katie's back and fastened the snaps. "There. Now all you need is the shoes and you're a clown."

"You didn't have to get all dressed up on my account." Matt's deep voice came from just over Katie's right shoulder.

Katie wanted to die. She wanted to dash over to the corner and curl up into a multicolored ball and stay there until closing time came and she could escape under cover of darkness. She wanted to do anything but turn around and face Matt clad in a clown suit and rainbow wig, after walking away from him last week, her head held high.

At least she hadn't put on the big floppy shoes.

"Hello, Matt. How nice to see you." She was a calm, cool and collected clown, but her heart was catapulting in her chest and her brain was shocking it with strong doses of reality. The chances of Matt reconsidering relationships and commitment were slim to none.

But hope washed over her anyway.

Oh, she had missed his smile. His touch. His eyes, and the way they crinkled in the corners when he laughed. The dimple under his chin…everything.

"Don't tell me," he said, "you've decided to run away and join the circus? Or do you have some secret fetish with fake hair and big shoes that I should know about?"

"Very funny," Katie said, tugging off the wig. Sarah was laughing so hard, she had to clutch her stomach.

But then just as quickly, the air in the room changed, like a wisp of spring blowing in. Sarah murmured an excuse about tending to some flowers, then slipped out of the room.

"I've missed you." Matt's voice was hoarse. He lifted a hand to touch her cheek. "Very much."

Knowing she shouldn't, but unable to stop herself, Katie leaned into the feel of his work-rough hand against her cheek. His eyes were as blue as the sky early in the afternoon before the sun fully blossomed.

Olivia's odd comment and the store's future were far from mind. All she saw, all she felt, was Matt.

I want him. The realization hit her squarely in the gut. *All of him. His mind, his soul.*

He'd captured a part of her heart already, this man with a tragic past and a half built house. It wasn't the intrigue of dating a bad boy, as he'd put it, it was the temptation of uncovering the layers of his soul, of finding out what had shaped and formed him.

Not that she didn't find his physical shape downright appealing, too. Every time he was around, fireworks launched themselves in her midsection, exploding bombs of desire that no fire extinguisher could douse.

Her reactions to his kiss, to his every touch, told her this man was powerful, captivating and dangerous. She needed to get involved with him about as much as she needed a hole in her head, as her mother would say.

She forced herself to pull away. "Did you stop by for some flowers?"

"No. I stopped by for you." Matt reached inside the pocket of his leather jacket and withdrew a small, wrapped box. "A peace offering," he said, handing it to her.

Katie tossed him a you-think-this-will-make-up-for-your-clown-joke look and took the gift. Even in the brightly colored clown suit, Katie was appealing. The tentlike outfit covered up every curve she had, but somehow, that made her more enticing. In his mind, he pictured what she looked like underneath the clown suit and whatever else she might be wearing. Bozo costume or not, those images ratcheted his pulse up a few notches.

He'd been unable to push her from his mind ever since he'd dropped her off at her apartment. He knew she was right to walk away, to stick to her own ethical code rather than get sucked into his slightly murky one by agreeing to a no-strings fling. And he knew he was wrong for being here, for trying to entice her back into his arms again.

But he couldn't help himself.

In one week, she'd managed to set fire to areas of his

body and, he had to admit, his soul, that had been nearly reduced to ashes. There'd been a couple of women over the years that he'd considered staying with after the sun rose. Invariably, though, he'd opted for the quick fix—the type of relationship that didn't last longer than the need to quench his bodily urges. He wasn't a glutton for punishment, and getting his heart stomped on once in his life was one time too many.

He suspected, no—he *knew*—that he could fall for Katie and fall hard. After he'd left her, he'd had to force himself to walk down the hallway and out the door instead of turning around and making promises he knew he couldn't keep. At that moment, minutes after tasting the sweetness of her lips, he would have said anything to bring her back.

"This isn't a red rubber nose, is it?" Katie took the ribbon off the box and began to tug off the wrapping paper. "Oh, Matt! Where did you find these?"

He didn't answer. He was too busy watching her smile spread across her face and light up her eyes. When she looked up at him, there was happiness reflected in the hazel depths. A tingle ran through him. He should make her smile more often. A lot more often.

Katie held up the tiny pair of enamel and gold earrings, letting them dangle from her fingers. They sparkled in the light. "I've never seen earrings in the shape of bananas before." She chuckled.

He didn't tell her he'd driven all the way into Indianapolis to shop for her, that he'd spent four hours looking at ordinary rings and ordinary necklaces until he'd finally happened upon the banana earrings in a small shop on the north side of the city. The salesclerk had eyed him suspiciously when he bypassed the traditional diamonds and sapphires, opting for the fruit-shaped novelty pair instead.

"They reminded me of you. I couldn't pass them up."

She unfastened the gold studs she wore on her lobes, replacing them with his gift. "What do you think?"

He picked one up in his fingers, the back of his hand drifting down her cheek. "Beautiful, absolutely beautiful."

She flushed and stepped back. His hand dropped away. "Thank you, Matt. They're lovely."

"Lovely?"

"Okay, delicious," she chuckled.

"And so are you. Delicious, that is." He tilted her head up and lowered his mouth to hers.

It was wrong to kiss her, wrong to keep intruding on her heart and body when he knew he wasn't going to hang around long enough to sort out the pieces when it was over between them. But he couldn't resist, couldn't ignore the urgent, pounding message his body was sending him.

"Matt, we shouldn't. We—"

"Shh," he whispered. "Just kiss me."

She hesitated for one agonizing second, then closed the gap between them and wrapped her arms around his back. When she did, a strange zing rippled through him. Coupled with the heady rush of desire that hurtled through his body as they kissed, the feeling surprised and amazed him.

If he'd been forced to name that feeling, he'd have to call it joy. That was something he hadn't felt in a long, long time.

His hands roamed along her back, rippling over the valleys of her spine. Her breasts fit perfectly in the space left by his opened jacket.

She murmured his name against his mouth and he nearly came undone. Their kiss turned wild, each of them gripped by a fever to taste and tempt the other. Mouths and tongues combined in a dance of desire that foreshadowed what could happen if they'd been in a bedroom instead of a cramped storage room.

A bell tinkled from somewhere in the front of the store and Katie broke away from him. "A…a…customer," she stammered. "It's not good for business to get caught necking in the back room."

A draft of cool air filled the space between them. Katie might as well have been ten miles away.

"We could neck quietly," he said, moving to take her in his arms again. "I promise, I won't make a peep." *Just let me kiss you again, just let me know that feeling one more time before you send me on my way.*

"No." She firmly pushed him away and turned toward the door. "Thank you for the earrings, Matt. They're exactly what I needed to complete my banana persona." Her tone was teasing, but the distance between them didn't disappear. "It was nice to see you again," she said. The happiness in her eyes, however, had been replaced by regret.

"Nice enough that you'll consider going out with me again? I have this wedding I was invited to and I'm not up to going without a date." He grinned.

She shook her head, and he felt disappointment shoot through him. Why did it matter whether this woman said yes? Why this woman, when there had been others before her who'd come and gone in his life like cars in a drive-through?

He lifted his hands in the air. "I promise, no touching, not even a kiss, if you don't want me to."

"Matt, I want to see you again, but—" She looked away, shaking her head. "But it would just delay the inevitable."

"Hey, we had a deal. You came through on your end of the bargain. Now, I'd like to repay you by escorting you to that wedding. Nothing more."

"You don't need to take me to the wedding. You've done enough. Business has picked up since the customers started coming in to talk about us."

"We've created a stir, have we?"

"More like a mini tornado."

"Then going to the wedding together will top the cake, if you'll pardon the pun. No one will ever call you conventional again." He traced a finger along her lip. "Although where you got that nickname, I'll never know. You're far from predictable."

Katie let out a breath. "You don't know me that well."

"Then let me take you to the wedding and work on getting to know you better."

"No, Matt." She lowered her head, paused, raised it again. "I know the ending of this story already. You're not looking for anything beyond tomorrow. I've already been down that road with someone else. I don't need another Steve."

Ouch. She knew just where to hit to make her point. And as much as he wanted to correct her, he knew she was right. In the end, he'd leave, too, and be no better than Steve.

"Katie—" He wanted to kiss her again, but didn't. There she stood, still clad in the clown suit, and all he could think about was taking her to bed and seeing what she looked like under the purple jumpsuit and pompoms.

"Thank you for the earrings." Her smile was bittersweet. "And thank you for showing me there's more to life than I ever knew."

Then she turned and left him there, wishing he could run after her and tell her she was all wrong about him.

But she wasn't. Katie had hit that nail on the head with precise accuracy.

Chapter Eight

St. Michael's Church loomed before Katie, sporting a steeple so tall, it practically brushed the underside of the clouds. It was a perfect Saturday—an exquisite setting sun, mild temperature with a hint of a breeze—just right for a wedding. And for a crazy idea that had seemed like a good plan early this morning—before coffee. What good was saying she'd moved on if she never showed it? Now, almost eight hours later, Katie wasn't so sure. Butterflies raged in her stomach and threatened to upheave her lunch.

It was the same church where she'd spent two of the most humiliating hours of her life. Now she was *volunteering* for mortification.

She thought of turning around and bolting for her car. But she was already halfway up the stairs, a smile pasted on her face to greet the people she knew. She'd been brought up to be friendly and gracious, no matter the circumstances. Her mother would burst with pride if she could see Katie now, being cordial all over the place.

A number of people nodded greetings at her, their eyes

full of surprise. Without missing a beat or tripping over her own two feet, Katie returned their hellos. If nothing else, Katie figured she'd gotten awfully good at pretending in the last year. She sent a wave to Carol Mullins, a friend from high school.

"Katie?" Carol, a tall woman in a Bohemian-style sundress, was almost gangly in her movements across the steps. "I thought that was you!"

"In the flesh." Katie paused on the top step. Her car had never seemed so far away.

"Congratulations! I'm so happy to hear about you and Matt Webster. I never knew—" Carol blushed. "Anyway, I think it's awfully big of you to come to Steve's wedding. I don't know many women who could do something like that."

Katie couldn't stand here and have a conversation about this. All she wanted to do was get in the church, make an appearance and leave. She murmured something and moved away, but Carol followed her, chattering about the weather or the decorations or something—Katie barely heard her.

She took a deep breath, then marched through the double doors and into the vestry. Two tuxedoed groomsmen flanked either side of the aisle leading into the sanctuary. "Bride's side or groom's?" one of them asked.

Neither. Faced with walking down that aisle, once again adorned with swooping pink ribbons and a roomful of hope, Katie balked. She couldn't do it. It had been a crazy idea.

"I need to go to the ladies' room," she stammered. Then she darted down the hall and away from all the happy faces and blooming flowers before anyone could stop her. Even in high heels, Katie found she could move pretty fast, given the right impetus.

The church was huge, filled with hallways and anterooms that offered more choices than a game show. It had been a year since she'd been inside St. Michael's, and, in her panic, she couldn't remember where anything was. She couldn't find the right door for the rest room—or a hiding place.

The organist began playing, the music booming through the building, reverberating in the walls. Just as Katie grasped a door handle, someone came bursting through it, nearly colliding with her.

She popped back in surprise. "Steve?"

He halted. Sweat beaded along his forehead and his breath was coming in gasps. "Katie! You came!" Then again, with more surprise, "You really came. I didn't think you would."

"You're here, too. That's a surprise."

He looked almost sheepish. "Yeah, I'm here. But I think I'm going to puke." He swiped a hand across his brow. "I was just looking for the restroom." He glanced toward the Exit. "I thought about leaving, about not even showing up. But I didn't."

"Why?"

"It's time I grew up."

Before she could stop herself, Katie blurted out the question that had lain in the back of her mind all this time. "Why couldn't you do that for me a year ago?"

"I was an idiot." Steve offered up the grin she'd fallen in love with, the one that asked her to forgive him and to love him, all at the same time. This time, she didn't. That smile had lost its power over her. "I mean, I always intended to stop running around and settle down with you, I really did. You were…well, you were good for me. It's just me who wasn't good for you."

Katie let those words hang in the air.

"I remember standing in my apartment that day, putting on my tux, and all I kept thinking was: One woman? For my whole life?" He shook his head. "I panicked. Barbara had stopped by to drop off a couple of gifts and…well, I guess you know the rest."

"Yeah, I do." She supposed she would have been justified if she yelled at Steve. But what would be the point now?

In Steve's eyes, she saw true regret and apology. "You're a good woman, Katie. I never appreciated that."

"Steve—"

"No, I mean it. I was wrong when I said you were boring and…" his voice trailed off as he searched for the words he'd flung at her in the letter he'd sent from Barbados.

"Predictable," she supplied. "Conventional. Frigid."

He cringed. "Yeah, I guess I said all that, too." He reached out a hand, as if he were going to touch her, then withdrew. "I'm really sorry. You deserved a lot better than what I gave you."

"Yeah, I did."

Steve cleared his throat and stepped toward the doors. "I should go. I'm still not sure about the one-woman-forever thing," he let out a shaky laugh, "but I'm going through with it."

"Because you love Barbara?"

He shrugged. "Who knows what love is? I sure as hell don't. My dad marries women and trades them in like used cars. I guess I inherited some of that from the old man. Permanence is not my thing, you know?" Steve ran a hand through his hair. "Barbara understands me. She's got the same kind of family. We're not banking on forever here. We're just trying it out."

The prelude of organ music swelled louder. Steve turned to Katie. "You'll be okay?"

She smiled. "Of course."

And then he was gone. She watched him leave, a trim, handsome man who filled the elegant tuxedo well, and realized the spark that had drawn her to him was gone. She was over him, over the whole betrayal. Ready to move on with someone else.

Then, as if he'd been drawn by telepathy, she heard Matt's voice. "Katie! I've been looking all over for you!"

Matt had come. Even though she'd told him twice not to, he'd shown up anyway. A rush of joy flooded Katie, but she held herself in check. Just because he was here didn't necessarily mean anything had changed. But maybe...

This rampage of emotion running through her at the sight of him had begun the night they'd played darts. Her single comment about there being a good man buried underneath his bad-boy exterior had dissolved his swagger and revealed the true Matt. It had touched her, as had his love for a beaten-up old farm, and the pain in his eyes when he talked of his baby.

Were these feelings...love?

No. There was no way she could be falling in love with Matt Webster.

But as he approached, she knew she was lying to herself. The truth came to her in a sudden punch that sucked out her air and compressed her lungs. She'd fallen in love with Matt. Irrevocably.

"Someone said you ran back here. Why?"

"I was..." She could barely talk. She was afraid the truth of how she felt about him would be reflected in the hesitation of her voice, in the shimmer of her eyes. She swallowed and tried again. "I was looking for an escape route."

"Escape, huh?" He wrapped his arms around her waist and drew her to him. Every touch felt different now, layered with meaning. Katie leaned into him, a bit unsteady on her feet. Inside, she could hear the beginning strains of Wagner's "Bridal Chorus."

"I think I can help you there," Matt said. He tipped his

head toward the window across the hall. "If you want, I can tie all my clothes together as a rope and lower you out the window." He put a finger to his chin. "I'd probably have to get naked to do that, though. Would you mind?"

She laughed. "I wouldn't complain."

His hands went to his belt buckle. "Well? Shall we?"

"I think that would be going above and beyond the call of duty here." Katie choked back her worries that Matt's arrival meant nothing more than he was bored on Saturday night. She gave in to the hope that maybe he was beginning to feel the same way she did. Mustering every bit of the new Katie, she leaned forward and pressed a kiss to his lips. "It was a sweet offer."

"No, *that* was sweet." He bent to kiss her again, then stopped. "I thought I heard Steve's voice earlier."

Did Matt look worried? Jealous? "You did."

"And has he...did he reconsider marrying Barbara?"

"No, he went through with it." Katie glanced toward the door that led to the church. "I'm not so sure he's making the right decision, but for once, he seems committed."

"Are you okay with that?"

She nodded. "I don't love him anymore. And if he loves Barbara, he should be with her."

"A happy ending for everybody, huh?"

Wagner reached the crescendo. "That's what I'm hoping for. Steve said he backed out of marrying me because he was terrified to commit to one woman for the rest of his life. Know anyone else like that?" She tugged on Matt's tie.

He feigned innocence. "You couldn't mean me. I'm not scared of anything, baby," he said in his best Schwarzenegger voice.

"Nothing?" She smoothed the navy silk back into place.

"Well…maybe black widow spiders and rogue building inspectors."

She tiptoed her fingers up his chest. "And you're not scared of me?"

"No, definitely not of you." He lowered his mouth to hers, hovering there, teasing her. "Are you scared of me?"

"Oh yeah. Terrified." And she surged forward, bringing her lips to his.

By the time they came up for air, Mendelssohn's "Wedding March" was playing and the new Mr. and Mrs. Stephen Spencer were dodging birdseed on their way to a waiting limo.

Matt and Katie dashed into the reception hall, laughing and holding hands like a couple of teenagers who'd just made out in the back seat of a car. The making out part was true, Matt thought. Tonight, though, he'd discovered how much fun the halls of a church and the front seat of a car could be.

When he'd decided to come to the wedding, despite Katie's protests, he'd thought he was doing it out of altruism. But the minute he'd seen her in the hall talking to Steve, and felt a powerful surge of something that seemed damned close to jealousy, he knew there was more to his decision than keeping a bargain.

They came up short when they nearly collided with a life-size papier-mâché Elvis. Not the handsome Elvis of "Love Me Tender," but the older, puffy white-suited King. Done in glue and paper, he looked more like the Pillsbury Dough Boy than the man who broke a million hearts.

The whole room was a tribute to Presley. Records served as place cards, stuffed hound dogs leashed to balloons were centerpieces. No less than eleven velvet Elvises adorned the pristine white walls of the exclusive Lawford Country Club.

"I always knew Barbara was an Elvis fan, but I never knew it went this far," Katie said.

"Speak of the devil," Matt whispered.

Barbara dashed over, clasping Katie's hands in her own. Or at least Matt thought it was Barbara. Her hair was done in a huge cloud on top of her head, her eyes rimmed with black and her lips coated with pale lipstick. If she hadn't been blond, she could have been Priscilla's clone. Matt wondered if a reporter from the *National Enquirer* was skulking behind the potted plants, hoping for an appearance of the King's ghost. If anything would make Elvis come back from the dead, it would be this party.

"Don't you just love it?" Barbara gushed. "It's always been my dream to have a true Elvis wedding, ever since I saw *Blue Suede Shoes.* I was so glad my mother already owned all these portraits of the King," she waved at the velvet Elvises with pride. "No trouble finding the decorations for this wedding!"

"It's…it's…unique," Katie said.

"Oh, thank you." She pressed a hand to her chest and beamed. Apparently, having legally snagged Steve in the setting of her dreams had Barbara feeling magnanimous instead of mean. "Well, you two enjoy yourselves, I've got to go see about the food. The chef wasn't too keen on the idea of serving peanut butter and banana sandwiches as an appetizer."

Barbara left, her hair like a beacon. Matt put a hand to the small of Katie's back and propelled her toward the bar. "In all the…ah…confusion back at the church," he grinned, "I forgot to tell you that you look incredible. The kind of beautiful that could make a weaker man's heart stop."

Even that wasn't enough to describe how wonderful she looked. The dress was a clear departure from what he'd seen

Katie in thus far. Ebony and silky, it lifted, tightened and enhanced all the right places, then flared out at the bottom. The best part was the scoop bodice, giving the illusion that Katie's breasts were ready to spill out with the first strong gust of wind. Unfortunate that the reception was inside, with little chance of a quick breeze.

"Thanks, I borrowed the dress from Sarah. You don't look so bad yourself." She ran a hand down the front of his suit jacket. "Presentable enough for a wedding."

He barely heard what Katie said, but noticed every detail about her. The delicate curve of her jaw, the way her lower lip pouted like a newly-budded apple. The slender fingers that slipped along his jacket with a feather touch, awakening a long-sleeping volcano of feeling. "Well," he cleared his throat. "I aim to please."

"I've noticed."

"And are you pleased?"

"With the clothes or the man?"

"The man." He tried to make it sound like he was joking. That her answer didn't mean anything.

She put a finger to her chin and feigned deep thought. "I guess I'd have to say both."

He smiled. "Then I'd better be on my best behavior tonight. Wouldn't want you realizing I'm not such a nice guy after all."

"I don't think that's going to happen."

"You don't know me that well," he said quietly. And there it was, the truth about the kind of man Matt knew he really was, slipping between them like a curtain. He could play this game of pretending there was hope for more, that he didn't have the past that he did, but in the end, it all came back to one night and one stupid, foolish choice. He ran a hand through his hair and forced himself back to the present. "So, where's the clown suit?"

"I thought this dress might be a bit more appropriate." She spun and the skirt swirled around her legs, à la Marilyn Monroe. All they needed was a rush of air from a subway grate and he'd get another glimpse of her fabulous legs.

"Too bad. I was really starting to get turned on by those orange pompoms."

"Someday, if you're really lucky, I'll wear the Bozo suit just for you," she said. There were layers of meaning, hints of tomorrow, in her words. Hope, then regret that those days would probably never come to pass, surged through him. Why had he come? Why had he thought that he could make a new life here in this town? He belonged in Pennsylvania, far from where his past lived.

No, you belong with Katie, his mind whispered. He let that thought simmer for a while.

They passed by the stage where the band, dressed in rhinestones and satin, was belting out "Blue Suede Shoes." At the mike, crooning and gyrating, was a rotund man wearing an Elvis wig and faux sideburns. "Look," Katie exclaimed. "That's Jim! The bartender at the Corner Pocket. He's Elvis!"

"Don't tell me the King has spent the last thirty years mixing drinks while everyone thought he was resting in peace."

She turned and flashed him a look of mock irritation. "If you keep up with these one-liners, I'm going to—"

"Punish me?" He winked. "That could get interesting."

"Matt Webster, you have the worst mind." She wagged a finger at him. "You're supposed to be pretending to be in love with me, not thinking up wild fantasies."

He grabbed her finger, pulled her to him. "Then come here," he whispered, "and let's start pretending right now." His arm slid around her waist possessively, his chest pressed against hers. The room slipped away, leaving nothing but Katie and him.

When they kissed, Matt forgot where the pretending left off and the reality began. He cupped her face, the soft skin a salve for his rough palms, as if the feel of her could heal the calluses on his hands and in his heart. His mind rocketed down a path of the future, first stopping with Katie in his bed, then Katie at his breakfast table, then seeing her on the porch at the house that he'd always dreamed of building and in her arms, their child, waving a grubby hand—

He yanked himself back. No, he couldn't have that. He didn't deserve any of it.

But God help him, he still wanted her. The dream. All of it.

"Matt? Are you okay?"

He didn't answer. What could he say? Instead, he looked for a distraction. The band announced a break and put on a CD of dance music to keep everyone entertained while they were gone. A sensual Latin rhythm began, pulsing through the floorboards and mocking the rock-and-roll theme of the room. Matt grabbed Katie's hand and dragged her to the center of the dance floor. "Let's give everyone something to talk about besides the decor."

"What do you mean? *Dance?*" She shook her head, already turning back to the sidelines. "I can't dance."

"You can with me." He placed her left arm along his right, so her hand rested on his shoulder. Then he took her opposite hand with his, angling them outward. "We're going to tango."

"You're kidding me. I can't—"

"Just follow my lead." He shifted his weight from foot to foot, without moving. "Do you feel that? Let my body cue you, not the music."

Did she feel that? Oh, yes, she certainly did. She felt *everything* when Matt was near.

Sarah's words about pretend love turning into real love echoed in her head. It had happened for her; maybe it could happen for Matt. Tonight was her best shot at making that happen. She'd met challenges before, head-on, with determination. Matt, though, was a challenge of a whole different sort. She didn't have the experience or know-how to wrap men around her finger the way other women did. In most areas of love, she was a novice.

On the dance floor, she was even more of an amateur. But she was still game, as long as Matt didn't let go. "Okay," she said.

"Now, lift your head, turn it slightly to the side and stay with me. Closer." He brought her chest to his, their torsos linked. "And think like a cat."

"Meow."

"Perfect."

He took a step back, pressing a hand to her spine to signal her move. She followed his lead, stepping forward, moving with him. He took another step back and again she followed.

It was almost like walking but deeper, more sensual. They moved to the rhythm, crossing the floor with an easy series of steps and follows. The music pulsed through Katie, giving her a natural tempo to obey. "Where did you learn to do this?"

"My mother insisted on a few lessons at Arthur Murray." He smiled. "I went because it was a great place to meet girls."

"Shouldn't I have a rose between my teeth?"

"No. That would make it hard for us to kiss. And what's a tango without a kiss or two?" He leaned forward and brushed her lips with his, a tease that caused a fire to erupt in her belly. She pressed against him. And promptly lost her footing.

"Easy there," he whispered. "Think cat, remember? Long, feline-type steps. Now get ready, we're about to turn. Don't worry, I'll make it easy for you."

He brought his palm tighter against her back and swooped her up off the floor, spinning her ninety degrees. She'd probably only been two inches off the ground but she felt light-headed. Her skirt was still swirling around her legs when he lowered her to her feet. She stumbled once, trying to get the hang of the steps again.

"*Feel* the music, Katie," he whispered to her. "For a tango to be done right, you have to pour yourself into the dance."

The music pounded a seductive beat that tingled through her, murmuring the promises of a bedroom later on. Katie slipped into the easy skin of what lay underneath the restrictions she'd placed on herself. She closed her eyes, letting instinct take over, embracing his body with her own. Every muscle he flexed, every movement he made, pulsed through him and into her. Close, closer still, she moved toward him, becoming one dancer, one person with Matt.

"Ah, Katie, Katie," Matt murmured against her neck. "I think I'm falling in love with you."

"I…I feel the same way about you," she whispered and let the joyful words carry themselves straight to her heart, no longer aware they were in a crowded room, no longer caring if the facade had worked.

The music came to an end, and, with one final swirl, Matt spun her around. She arched her back and flung out an arm, the triumphant dancer finishing the finale of her life. Matt dropped to one knee, clasping her free hand in his.

Applause erupted from the sidelines. When Katie opened her eyes, she realized they were the only people on the dance floor. The entire crowd of nearly one hundred people had gathered around and watched as she and Matt danced.

She knew then that the Conventional Katie moniker was gone for good. And best of all, Matt had said he was falling in love with her. Hope for a future with him sprang to life in her chest, blossoming into a wide smile. She couldn't remember ever feeling this happy.

Matt got to his feet and grasped her waist, bowing with her to another round of applause. "We put on one hell of a good show, according to the audience," Matt said.

"Yes, we did."

"I think they really believed our performance." He looked down at her. She smiled back, letting the happiness brim over and no longer holding back the truth. But then a shadow passed over his face, dropping onto his features like a shade. Matt took a step back. Cold air invaded the space between them. "That little touch I added about saying I was falling in love worked wonders."

His words lanced through her. Hot, painful tears stung at her eyes and a crushing weight she could barely swallow sunk to the pit of her stomach. "Yeah, I…I guess it did," she managed. "You're a great actor."

He looked away. "So are you."

"Thanks." The word came out flat, stale. For the last few minutes, she'd been letting herself hope that maybe he wasn't pretending. That he hadn't said he was in love with her just because it was part of their bargain…but because he really did.

"I've accomplished what I wanted," she said, trying to hold the tears in check long enough to get out of the room. "After a finale like that, I think I should go home."

"Are you sure? We could always try the foxtrot—"

"No. No, I've had enough." She put on her cordial face

again, said goodbye to the people she knew and hurried out the door as fast as she could, away from Matt. She'd thought no one could ever hurt her the way Steve had.

She'd been wrong. So very, very wrong.

Chapter Nine

Matt caught up to her in the country club lobby. "Katie—"

She spun around. "Thank you for putting on a great show. The whole act was very convincing."

He heard the forced brightness in her tone and knew exactly what had upset her. How could he be so stupid? How could he let his feelings get away from him like that? He'd told her he was falling in love with her and then he'd taken it back.

What had he been thinking? He hadn't been, and that was the trouble. He'd let himself get swept up in the dance and in Katie, and the words had slipped out. He'd been reacting on emotion, not with his head. "Katie, I—"

Before Matt could finish his sentence, Olivia came striding around the corner. She was holding color swatches in her hands and chatting with a man who looked to be the manager of the country club. When she saw Matt, she froze. "I'll, ah, catch you later, Stan," she said to the man beside her. He took one look at Matt, another at Olivia and Katie, and left without a word.

Olivia looked the same as ever, Matt thought, but a little older and harder. She was thin, almost painfully so, and there were lines in her face that hadn't been there eleven years ago. Maybe the last decade hadn't been so easy on her, either.

"Matt," Olivia said. The word came out in a quiet gush of surprise.

"Hello, Olivia."

"I knew you were in town, but…" She didn't finish. Instead, she turned to Katie, as if she'd just noticed she was there. Olivia's features went stony, yet her voice remained cool. "I didn't expect to see you two together—I mean, I heard about…but…" She recovered and put on a polite face. "Nice to see you, Katie."

"And you," Katie said. She took an almost imperceptible step away from Matt. "Olivia has ordered some designs from my shop," Katie told Matt.

That explained the distance Katie put between them. Never get in the middle of a man and his ex-wife, Matt thought wryly. "What a small world."

"Indeed," Olivia said. An uncomfortable silence curled around them until Olivia held up the swatches and waved them vaguely toward the lounge. "I was here to go over a few details for the renovation. Are you here for a something special?"

"A wedding," Katie said.

"Not your own?" Her laughter seemed forced.

"No, no." Katie shook her head. "A friend's."

"Oh. Well, it was nice to see you again, Katie." Olivia nodded at Matt. "Are you in town long?"

Seeing Olivia magnified all the guilt and anger brewing in Matt. He tried to cram it back into the recesses of his heart, but he couldn't. The feelings he'd managed to more or less put away for the past eleven years refused to go quietly. They kept bobbing up, forcing him to acknowledge them. To deal with them.

He was through running away and hiding from the past. He needed to find out the rest of the story. Maybe that would give him the peace he needed to move forward. Or maybe it would send him spiraling off a steeper cliff of self-blame.

"We have some unfinished business, Olivia," he said. "I'd like to talk—"

Olivia's face paled ten shades. "I have to go." She spun on her heel and left.

Olivia wasn't happy about his return, that was clear. His being with Katie hadn't been welcome news, either. What had Katie said? Olivia was using Katie's shop for some floral work. Damn. He hoped that his being with Katie hadn't hurt her business. He knew she and Sarah were struggling to keep it afloat.

But what could he say to Olivia? *It's all an act? We were just pretending so people would change their ideas of who Katie Dole and Matt Webster really are?* Olivia would never believe it.

His return had stirred up a hornet's nest of a mess. His parents were unhappy with his actions, his ex-wife had more than one resentment left, and his best intentions may have sent Katie's store further into financial trouble. And to top it all off, he'd just broken Katie's heart.

Way to go, Matt.

"I need to get home. I, um, have an early day tomorrow," Katie said.

"I thought the shop was closed on Sundays."

She flushed. "It is. But I have some things to do." She started out the door, heading toward the parking lot. Matt hurried after her, but he had a feeling that in her mind, she'd already left him.

"Thanks for the dance," Katie said when she reached her car. "It was a lot easier than nailing in two-by-fours. So, now we're even." She put out her hand. "And thanks for keeping your end of the bargain and putting on a good performance."

"This is how you want to end our night, with a handshake?"

"Yes. We're friends, right? Friends shake."

"I thought we were much more than friends."

"No, not really." But the lie shimmered in her eyes.

Damn, he had screwed up royally. How could he begin to mend the ever-widening rift between himself and Katie? He took her hand, but she pulled it away. "Katie—"

She shook her head. "I'm really tired."

"Katie, please, let's go get something to eat and then we can talk." He had no idea what he'd say if she agreed. All he knew was that he couldn't let her leave thinking he was the world's biggest jerk. Even if it was true. "Hey, and afterwards," he offered her what he hoped was a charming, irresistible smile, "we could tango a little more."

"It was all a charade, Matt." Her voice was thin and shaky. "You pretended, I pretended. Everyone fell for it. Bravo." She clapped her hands together.

Then she turned, got into her Toyota and pulled away before Matt could say the words that would make her stay.

"So? How was the wedding?" Sarah said when she breezed in Monday morning.

"It was nice." *Liar.*

Katie focused her attention on the partially completed silk flower arrangement on her workbench. It was easier to concentrate on the perfect place for the faux orchid in her hand than to think about Saturday night and about Matt. She'd worked all weekend, letting cleaning and organizing be her excuse for avoiding Matt and her thoughts. A hearty scrub of the bathtub, two passes over the kitchen floor and even a thorough dusting of the ceiling fan hadn't rid her system of him. Nothing had.

Sunday, her phone had rung twenty times and she'd ignored it every time. Twice, he'd come to the door and begged her to let him in. She'd turned up the volume on her stereo and pretended she couldn't hear him. The last thing she wanted to hear right now was Matt congratulating her again on a performance well done.

"Come on, give. I know it was more than 'nice.' I can tell by your face that something happened. Did Barbara abandon Steve at the altar?"

"No, but Steve looked like he was about ready to pass out. He went through with it, though. He even apologized to me for being such a jerk before."

"It's about time." Sarah leaned against the counter. "That delivery I need to get over to the Robertsons' house for their new baby can wait a few more minutes. Tell me, what happened with Matt?"

Katie sighed and gave up on the orchid. She'd bent the stalk in half by jabbing it too hard. She flung it onto the worktable and dropped her head to her hands.

"Katie." Sarah laid a hand on her shoulder. "What is it?"

She'd thought she didn't have any tears left. But she did. "Matt and I tangoed, he told me he was falling in love with me, then he compliment me on our great performance." She sniffled.

"Oh, Katie." Sarah grabbed a handful of tissues out of the box beside them and handed the stack to Katie. "But, he did say 'falling in love,' right?"

She nodded, swiping her eyes. "He also said it was an act."

"Hmmm." Sarah tapped a finger on her chin. "I don't think so. I think maybe Matt let something slip out that he didn't even realize he felt yet."

"Sarah, the man was pretending to be my fiancé, because we had a deal. Period. He doesn't love me. He doesn't even want a relationship." Katie picked up another flower. "It gets worse."

"Worse?"

"On the way out of the country club, Matt and I ran into Olivia Maguire. She wasn't too happy to see me with him. In fact, I wouldn't be surprised if she canceled her order."

"Looks like you're right about that one." Sarah gestured toward the door. Through the glass, Katie could see Olivia getting out of her car. Her heart sank.

"I'll stay. Maybe we can talk her out of canceling, if that's what she's here for."

"Go deliver that arrangement. I'll be fine."

Sarah hesitated. "Are you sure? I hate to leave you—"

"*Go.*"

"Okay. Good luck." Sarah gathered Katie in a quick, strong hug, then headed out the back door.

A moment later, Olivia entered the store. "I've decided to cancel the dish garden order," she said.

Dread filled Katie's lungs.

"Although I'm impressed with your work, certain circumstances have made me rethink our business relationship."

"I can assure you—"

"I've got a lot of work coming up, you know," Olivia interrupted. "Three houses, the country club, a new restaurant that's opening in Lawford." She ticked them off on her fingers. "All of these customers could use flowers. Some on a regular basis. I had intended to use your shop. Before I do, however, I want to make sure business is your *top* priority. I'd thought it was before, but now…'' She didn't finish.

''What do you mean, 'top priority?'''

''It's been my experience that small shops sometimes close unexpectedly when the owner finds something else to occupy her time.''

Katie knew precisely where this conversation was leading. ''Like a man?''

''I'm not saying that exactly, but yes, sometimes getting involved with someone or getting married becomes a, shall we say, a distraction. Then the shop isn't there when I need it most.''

''Does this have anything to do with me dating your ex-husband?''

''Of course not.'' But the flush that crept over Olivia's face contradicted her words. She sounded angry, and yet she looked a bit worried. Anger, Katie could understand. But worry?

''I don't want to commit to a business relationship with your shop right now. Maybe in a few weeks…''

When Matt was out of her life, was the implication. Katie was about to tell Olivia that it was already over between them, when she was caught by a thought. What did it matter to Olivia if Katie and Matt dated? The other night, she'd seemed to already know, from the growing scuttlebutt around town, that they were an item. And yet, until today, she hadn't said a word or threatened to hold back business from the shop.

Then Katie remembered Matt's comment to Olivia about wanting answers. Olivia had paled and run out of the country club. Like someone with something to hide.

Maybe there was a lot more to Olivia's part in the tragedy

about their baby's death and their divorce, than anyone knew. Was Matt blaming himself for something that wasn't his fault?

"I realize there might be some bad feelings between you and Matt," Katie ventured.

Olivia snorted. "Of course there are."

"It's been eleven years. It seems to me that's a long time to be—"

"Devastated? Betrayed?" Olivia took a step closer. "From what I've heard, you know a lot about feeling betrayed yourself. Being dumped at the altar is *nothing* compared to what I went through." She blinked, a glimmer of tears in her eyes. "So don't start telling me when it's time to get over it."

"I wasn't, I just…" Katie sighed.

"Let's drop the subject. It's not one of my favorites." With shaking fingers, Olivia whisked an invisible piece of dust off her cranberry suit. "I'm late for an appointment. I'll be in touch *if* I need your shop's services again." She strode out the door, letting it shut with a slam.

The air in the room seemed to descend like a heavy blanket. The glove had been thrown down by Olivia. She'd made it clear that involvement with Matt put far more than Katie's heart in jeopardy—it also threatened the store. Katie's priority, ahead of any relationship, any man, had to be the shop. She and Sarah both depended on it for income.

Katie slumped into a chair. She'd ruined everything. Olivia had no intention of giving any more business to A Pair of Posies. She seemed intent on distancing herself from Matt, and by extension, Katie.

Still, something nagged at Katie about the whole conversation. Certainly, Olivia and Matt had suffered a great loss when their child had died. But why was she still so inflamed by the subject more than a decade later?

Sarah returned, waving a check. "The family was so pleased with the arrangement, they ordered a silk version for the nursery."

Katie scrambled to her feet and grabbed her car keys off the ring by the register. "That's great. Listen, I need to take care of something. Will you be all right here alone for a little bit?"

"Sure. But before you go, tell me how it went with Olivia."

"Not good at all." Katie pushed on the door handle. "But I'm about to try and fix that."

"Dammit!" Matt yanked on the tie at his neck, pulling out his misguided attempt at a Windsor knot for the third time. "You'd think I'd never tied a tie before in my life," he muttered.

He'd bought two of the damned things to wear with his equally new suit for the wedding. It had taken him nearly thirty minutes to get the first one on that night, and his skills hadn't improved. He doubted Katie would be impressed if he wrapped it around his neck in one enormous ball. His idea was to show up at her store, dressed to the nines—since that had seemed to please her last time—and persuade her to go out on a date with him. A real one this time.

He yanked out the bulging knot again and wondered if it was possible for a tie to have a mean streak.

"Do you want some help with that?" His mother appeared at his side, startling him. She had always moved silently through the house, a feat Matt had yet to accomplish. It must have something to do with his big feet, a physical characteristic definitely not inherited from his mother.

"I'm all thumbs today." He turned and faced her, giving

up on the irritating piece of silk. He felt ten years old again, waiting for his mother to help him get ready for church.

"Your father isn't so good at ties, either." She deftly looped the fabric in and around in the classic knot. "I've tied his every morning for forty-one years. It's a ritual with us."

That was something he hadn't known. His parents were not people who went through the daily intimacies of zipping back zippers and tying ties. They were companions who shared small talk over croissants and fresh-squeezed orange juice. He'd hardly seen them kiss, and certainly didn't want to imagine how he had come to be.

Ever since he'd been back, he'd been learning things about his parents, and about himself, that shocked the hell out of him. Now that he was thirty, and presumably older and wiser, he realized he'd been wrong about a few things.

"Are you going to see that Katie you told me about?" She tugged and tightened, straightening the knot. They'd talked about Katie on Sunday, when his mother had asked what had him stalking around the house like a penned lion.

"Yes. And, I hope, convince her I'm not a total jerk."

"You like her, don't you?"

He dipped his head and met her gaze. "Yes, I do. She's…special."

"Hmm," was all she said. Then she finished fastening the tie and patted it lightly. "There, all handsome now." Her hand moved up to stroke his cheek. "You look so much like your father did when I first met him." Her eyes glistened and there was a catch in her voice. "I think you ended up with the best of both of us, Matthew."

The best of each of them? That was something he'd never considered and the implications of her remark warmed him. He had to clear his throat before he could speak. "Thank you, Mom."

She brushed a lock of hair off his forehead and smiled. "You always were my little devil, running off, hell-bent on some idea or another. I never could keep you pinned down for long. Much like your dad."

"There was so much of the world to see, so many things to do."

"And after you saw the world and did all those things, you came home." She hesitated. "To stay?"

He nodded. "There are some things here that I never found anywhere else in the world." *Like Katie.*

She nodded, as if she'd read his mind. "Katie seems to be good for you."

Matt turned to the mirror and fiddled with the tie. She might be good for him. But he knew sure as hell he was no good for her.

As much as he hoped for a different ending, he was enough of a realist to know it wasn't possible. He could try to delay it by taking her to dinner, by seeing her one last time, but once she realized the truth about that night eleven years ago, she'd reject him as surely as his father had, blame him like Olivia did. Like he blamed himself.

Sweet Pea lay on the porch, snoring. The giant dog was sprawled across the top step and didn't even bother to pick her head up when Katie stepped over her to reach the front door and ring the doorbell. "You're quite the guard dog," she said to the Doberman.

Sweet Pea grunted and went back to her puppy dreams.

"Whatever you're selling, I ain't buying," Miss Tanner shouted before she'd finished opening the door. "Oh, it's you."

Katie stood firm on the porch. Miss Tanner had always been a formidable woman, and seemed even more so now, with her hair drawn into a severe bun and a broom in her hand. "I'd like to talk to you about something, Miss Tanner. Do you have a few minutes?"

"I'm in the middle of cleaning…"

Katie pulled out her trump card. "I brought some donuts along." She held up a bag, opened it and withdrew one of the sweet confections. "And a cruller for Sweet Pea."

The dog scrambled to her feet, nails clicking on the wood, and lunged for the cruller, snapping half of it off. Katie let out a squeak and dropped the rest of the donut on the porch, where it was promptly gobbled up by Sweet Pea.

"Donuts?" Miss Tanner leaned forward, peering into the bag. "Well, I guess I could use a break. For a few minutes." She opened the door wide enough for Katie to enter. Sweet Pea stayed on the porch, licking up every last crumb.

The inside of Miss Tanner's house was nearly as severe as the woman—and her mother before her, from what Katie had heard about the family. Though Miss Tanner had never married, the rumor mill said she'd spent a few years "abroad" before coming back at twenty-one. She'd never left again. There'd been plenty of gossip about why Miss Tanner had become almost a recluse.

The house didn't offer many clues. The front parlor had uncomfortable-looking furniture precisely arranged, white walls devoid of art or pictures. Then Miss Tanner led Katie into the kitchen. It was like a different house. Katie got the feeling this room was where the true spirit of Colleen Tanner existed.

The room was warm and bright, imbued with blue and yellow. A checked tablecloth, topped by a vase of fresh daisies, sat on the table. There was a stew simmering on the stove, and prints of flowers hung on the pale yellow walls. There was even a dog treat jar, painted to look like an enormous, fat pug.

"Sit down." Miss Tanner gestured to a kitchen chair. She

crossed to the sink, filled a kettle and placed it on the stove. "I'll make some tea." She bustled back with a pair of plates and napkins.

When Miss Tanner took a seat, Katie pushed the bag over to her. "They're all for you."

"Wonderful!" she crowed, digging in eagerly. "What did you want to ask?" She took a bite of a devil's food donut.

"About Olivia. And Matt."

Miss Tanner dropped the donut to her plate. Her entire demeanor shifted away from friendly. "I don't want to talk about that man. He broke my niece's heart after they lost the baby."

"It was an awful tragedy. So unexpected," Katie said, hoping Miss Tanner would fill in a couple of blanks.

"The women in our family are cursed." Miss Tanner shoved the donuts away as if the conversation had killed her appetite. "Cursed in the men they marry, cursed with their babies."

"What do you mean?"

"There isn't a one of us who hasn't had that fear, seen that loss. Or had it happen to us." Miss Tanner's voice was quiet, her gaze off in the distance somewhere. Katie realized one of the women Miss Tanner meant was herself. No wonder she'd been so protective of Olivia, so angry at Matt. Whatever had happened, had also happened to the woman across the table. "Olivia thought she might escape the curse, but she was wrong."

"What curse?"

The tea kettle whistled and Miss Tanner shuddered. The softness left her features and she became the bitter woman Katie normally saw. She shoved away from the table and turned to the stove, silencing the kettle. "Nothing I need to be telling you about," she said. "It's family business."

"I didn't mean to pry."

"Stay away from that man." She shook a wrinkled finger at Katie. "Mark my words, he'll break your heart like he broke Olivia's. Men aren't worth the skin they're grown in." She got to her feet, clearly done with Katie's visit. "I have work to do."

There was nothing more to be said. Katie suspected even a truckload of donuts wouldn't change Miss Tanner's mind.

"I need to get back to the store, anyway." Katie said as she headed down the hall, Miss Tanner close on her heels. Miss Tanner reached past Katie, opened the door and waited.

Katie had failed on her mission. She'd hoped to unearth some deep family secret and all she'd gotten was something about a curse and a few choice words about how useless men were. So far, the new Katie was batting a thousand.

"Thank you, Miss Tanner," she said.

Miss Tanner harrumphed. "For what?"

"For inviting me into your house. And for telling me a little more about Olivia. I'm sure it wasn't easy to talk about."

Miss Tanner looked taken aback. Surprised. Actually bordering on nice. "No, it's not." She dipped her gaze, but not before Katie saw her eyes mist. "The same thing happened to my baby, God rest his soul. And my sister's second child, who would have been Olivia's younger brother. The girls in our family ain't meant to have sons." Miss Tanner cleared her throat and straightened, her gaze scanning the sky. "It looks like rain."

It didn't, but Katie agreed anyway. She said goodbye and stepped over Sweet Pea on her way out. The dog lifted her head in a drowsy farewell.

Miss Tanner's confession about her baby certainly made many of the rumors about her time "away" add up. Had she gotten pregnant and then been abandoned by the baby's father? That, coupled with the loss of a child, must have been hard. Miss Tanner's honesty, though, might just set another person free of a lifetime of pain.

There was only one place Matt would be right now, Katie decided. Mustering every bit of her new self, she took a chance and headed for the man who'd just broken her heart.

Chapter Ten

The new suit no longer looked new. Matt had draped the tie over a pile of lumber, tossed the jacket onto a sledge-hammer handle. His pants and shoes were coated with sawdust; the shirt plastered to his skin in a wrinkled, sweaty mess.

He probably should have changed before coming out to the house. But when he'd reached Katie's store, only to find out she wasn't there, he'd needed a place to vent his frustration. He hadn't thought about what he was wearing—all he wanted was the familiar feel of a hammer in his hands. It was either work or beer, and he wasn't about to go down the beer path again.

He dragged a pair of two-by-tens over to the bearing wall he was creating. He parked his wing tip against the two of them, keeping them in place, then bent forward and drove a ten-penny galvanized nail into the wood.

"Nice view."

For a second, he didn't move. Was that Katie's voice?

Damn, he sure hoped so. The hammer dropped to the floor with a clatter and Matt spun around. "Hey."

Way to go, Matt. Nice loss for words.

"Hey yourself." She gestured toward the wood. "Need some help?"

"Uh, yeah. Sure." He had the vocabulary of a Cro-Magnon man. "You're not really dressed for it, though."

She chuckled. "Neither are you."

He shrugged. "I forgot to change."

She reached into her bag and pulled out a bottle of soda. It was covered with a thin layer of frost. "I brought you something to drink."

He took the bottle, ran the icy container between his hands. "Thank you. Is this why you stopped by?"

"No. I have something to tell you."

Hope sparked within him. "What?"

"Olivia came by the shop earlier. She canceled her order." Katie frowned. "She seemed extremely angry and more than a little worried about seeing me with you. That bothered me, so I went to see Miss Tanner. She told me something interesting about Olivia."

Matt turned away. "I told you, I don't want to talk about her."

"Matt." Her voice was soft. "You can't let what happened that night rule the rest of your life."

He wheeled back. "Yeah, I can. You don't know me very well. You don't know how badly I can disappoint people."

She glanced away, and he remembered she'd already had a taste of that from him, too. He was lower on the evolutionary scale than Cro-Magnon man. Even a caveman wouldn't lash out at a woman who wasn't doing anything wrong.

"I shouldn't have said that." He twisted the cap off the

bottle but didn't drink. "Damn it, Katie. You don't understand. Nobody does. What happened that night—"

"Might not have been your fault."

"What are you talking about?"

"Miss Tanner said something that made me think there might be more to what happened than you know. Did Olivia ever mention a curse?"

"Curse?"

"Well, that's what Miss Tanner called it. But I think she meant something genetic. She told me her own infant had died, and so had her nephew, Olivia's baby brother. Then she said something about how the women in her family weren't meant to have sons."

"I remember Olivia telling me about her little brother," Matt said. He set the bottle on a post, still untouched. "But she told me he was stillborn. What happened to the other babies?"

Katie shook her head. "I don't know. Miss Tanner didn't tell me anything else."

He crossed to a pile of lumber and took a seat. Katie laid a hand on his shoulder. "Matt, was there an autopsy?"

"I…I don't know," Matt said. "I left town after the hospital told me it was SIDS. I couldn't bear to be there one more second."

"You're blaming yourself for something that probably isn't even your fault."

"What Miss Tanner said doesn't change what I did. Blaming Olivia won't—" He leapt to his feet. "There are things about me, about my past, that you don't know."

"Matt, the past—"

"Will affect the future." He lowered his head. "Maybe once I tell you, you'll understand why relationships and me are a bad idea."

"Okay." She took a seat on the stack of lumber. He

paced for several minutes before finally settling beside her. He steepled his fingers under his chin, hesitating.

Katie waited quietly. Any other woman would have been nagging and cajoling him. Katie wasn't any woman, though. In the hazel depths of her eyes, he saw the reflection of concern. Of caring. Maybe even the beginnings of love.

Already, he had a feeling he was in too deep. Like a hummingbird anxious about staying too long in one place, the thought of settling down flitted through his mind. Just being near her, in this house where hope used to live, was making him consider things he'd written off long ago— those age-old words every man pranced around like a race-horse just before the gate opened—commitment and marriage.

He'd been in that starting gate once before, with Olivia. The end of his marriage, which had really begun the day he'd slipped the ring on Olivia's finger, had been an avalanche of hurt. What he'd learned from that experience should be included in every boy's puberty handbook—how not to be seduced by a woman who lied as easily as she smiled.

He looked out over the property. Why had he started building again? Why had he laid out framing for four bedrooms instead of one? If he intended to live here by himself, in some self-imposed exile from society, then why four bedrooms?

The reason was sitting quietly beside him. Katie had given him the first taste of hope he'd had in a long time. Katie was right. Until he dealt with that night, hope was a wasted emotion.

"Olivia was my date for the senior prom," he began, letting the taste of long-bottled-up words roll off his tongue like a wine that had grown slightly bitter with age. "I didn't know many girls. Believe it or not, I got tongue-tied every time I got around a pretty girl and hadn't dated, even by my senior year.'' He flicked a splinter of wood onto the floor. ''She worked at the diner where my friends and I hung out. My buddies thought it would be funny to set us up, so they told her I didn't have a date for the prom. It didn't take long for her to change that.'' He shook his head.

''I used to think she and I had a lot in common. A poor girl from the wrong side of the tracks and a wild rich boy who didn't value money, just freedom. After we got married, I realized the *only* thing Olivia cared about was money and status. Me, I've never cared much about those things.''

She shook her head. ''I can't remember a time when I haven't worried about money.''

''I'm not against money in general,'' he said with a grin. He reached out, grabbed his soda off the nearby post and took a long gulp. ''I've just never wanted the lifestyle my parents had. The country club memberships, the agonizing over china patterns. Spending your life chained to a desk. I've worked for enough to live on, pay my crew well and save for the future. Money hasn't been my all-consuming goal, which ironically, seemed to make my business do better. When I worried more about the quality of the job than the cash we were making, customers respected me.''

''And for Olivia it was different?''

''Oh yeah. She thought that by marrying me, she'd taken care of for the rest of her life. I made sure she was, even after the divorce. Money buys the only security she can count on.'' He twirled the bottle in his palms.

''What happened at the prom?''

''It wasn't what happened at the prom, it was what happened afterward. We had a great time. Olivia was every guy's dream date—sexy, flirty, laughing. Ready to do just about anything. And I mean anything. After the prom, we were supposed to follow my friends up to the lake for a campout. But we didn't make it.''

The wind picked up, flattening the grass in a wave across the meadow. A few birds squawked in protest at the gust and flapped away.

"We ended up in a hotel room instead.''

Matt looked at Katie, as if gauging her reaction to the statement. She shouldn't have a reaction, she told herself. His relationship with Olivia had been eleven years ago, long before Katie had met him. On top of that, she had no claims on him, no right to be bothered by whatever had been or still was between Matt and Olivia.

But the thought of him and Olivia in bed together, did bother her. More than she wanted to admit.

"Olivia wanted me and made no secret of that the whole way to the hotel,'' he continued. "I was young, stupid and desperate to lose my virginity. So I went.''

"And the rest is history,'' she finished for him, not sure she wanted to hear any more details.

"Basically, yes.'' He glanced at the bottle in his hands. "Four weeks later, she called me, said she was pregnant and I was the father. Like I said, I was young and stupid. I believed her.''

"And you did the right thing.''

He nodded. "We got married a week later, to prevent any scandal, you know.'' Sarcasm laced his words. "My father was enraged that I could be so 'irresponsible.'''

"Did you live with your folks after the wedding?''

Matt laughed, a short dry sound that was anything but merry. "No way. I got a job working on a construction crew and rented an apartment downtown. I wasn't about to take a handout from my parents for a mistake I'd made and then hear about it until the day I died. I did it on my own.''

"And Olivia? How did she take it?''

"She hadn't expected that I'd *choose* to struggle by on my own rather than take money from my father. She never stopped complaining, not from the minute I carried her over the threshold. So I worked two jobs, until I could afford this place."

"To build her dream house."

He was looking past her, at some nameless spot far across the skeleton of a room. "At the time, I thought it would be *our* dream house. The one we'd raise our family in."

Matt's gaze swept over the framework of the house, lingering on a corner that faced the meadow.

"What happened?"

He took a long, hard gulp of soda. Then another, draining the bottle. "Then the baby died and everything fell apart." He spoke so softly, she had to strain to hear him.

"And you left town?"

"Basically." He nodded. Again, she waited, sensing his need to tell the story in his own time. "When I woke up on my thirtieth birthday, I finally realized what I'd given up. I'd run from this place as fast as I could eleven years ago and stayed away because it was...easier. But that day, it hit me that the memories I'd left behind, the life I'd had, meant more to me than I wanted to admit." He let out a rueful laugh. "I decided it was finally time to grow up and come home."

"But what about your construction company?"

"That can come with me, too, in a way. I built it up from scratch in Pennsylvania and I can do it again here. The challenge will be fun."

"Starting all over again takes a lot of courage."

He shook his head. "I wouldn't call myself courageous. Not at all." He stared at the lush landscape. "I'm just a man who stopped drinking and saw his life a whole lot clearer when he decided to face it head-on instead of running from it.''

"But you gave up an awful lot, to come back to a town that's always thought the worst of you." Katie laid a hand on his shoulder. "I think you did the right thing."

The right thing. He hadn't done the right thing in so long, he wasn't even sure he knew what that might be. He knew what the wrong thing was, though—choosing booze over responsibility. He'd lost his child, his wife and his life, all in one fell swoop. Then he'd turned his back on everyone and left, drowning his guilt alone.

He pushed himself to his feet and crossed to where the plywood floor ended. He teetered, balancing on the edge of the foundation. The wind gusted around him, as if trying to knock him down.

"Matt, tell me about the baby." Katie had joined him on the edge and drawn one of his hands into both her own.

"He was beautiful," Matt began, feeling each word before letting it escape. "Absolutely perfect. I was so happy when he was born. I handed out cigars to the entire staff on the maternity ward, even the candy stripers. *My* name was on his bassinet. Damn, that made me proud. I'd point him out to everyone that walked by the nursery: 'That's my son, that's my boy.' " He gestured in front of himself, the movement a mimic of the memory.

"Olivia wanted to name him after me," he added, turning toward Katie. "Did you know *Matthew* means 'gift of the Lord?' That's what he was, a precious gift that I had to give back much too soon." Then his voice splintered with grief and he had to stop talking.

Despite all that had happened, despite the letter proving it was all a lie, Matt had never stopped thinking of little Matthew as his son. A nest of wasps stung at his heart whenever he said his son's name. Would the pain ever stop?

Katie took a step closer, her warmth a buffer against the bite of the wind. "He must have made you very happy."

"I can't describe how that baby made me feel. It was like walking on clouds and touching the sun every time he smiled." Matt shook his head, regained the composure that had momentarily slipped out of his grasp. "I know they say it's just gas at that age, but I thought he knew who I was."

"I'm sure he did."

"When we brought him home from the hospital, everything was fine at first. Olivia and I spent hours talking about his toes or his eyes or how much he'd eaten." Matt rubbed a hand over his face and sighed. "But then Olivia started spending every night out. As soon as I'd get home from work, she'd head out the door and leave me with the baby."

"That must have been hard."

"Not really. I didn't mind taking care of my son. I used to go crazy while I was at work, missing him. I'm sure I drove the crew nuts, talking about him as if he were the first baby ever born in the world."

"For you, he was."

Matt glanced at her and nodded. "You're right."

Dark clouds pushed their way through the sky, casting the land in shadow. In the distance, the sound of a tractor droned an undertow of sound for the soft chirps of birds.

"Why didn't Olivia stay home?"

"She didn't know what to do when he cried. She'd get frustrated when she couldn't comfort him or he wouldn't sleep on schedule. I think she felt like a bad mother."

"You two were young. No wonder it was difficult."

"Olivia wouldn't talk about it or accept any help. Her parents died when she was young, so my mom would come over and try to help her out. But Olivia wanted to do it on her own. And when she couldn't, she'd get aggravated and walk out the door.

"My marriage was falling apart, bit by bit, and I couldn't stop it." He let out a breath. "When I married Olivia, I was committed to making it work—for the baby's sake. And so was she, in the beginning. But the more inadequate she seemed to feel as a mother, the more unhappy she'd become. Then she'd leave."

The wind whipped Katie's hair around her face. "Where do you think she went?"

"I didn't know at first. Later, I found out she was with another man. Jacob Cartland, a lawyer from the city. She'd known him before me and never really stopped seeing him. Whenever Olivia disappeared, she headed to his lake cabin. Cartland's wife didn't know a thing. She thought he hunted a lot."

"Why cheat? I thought she cared about you."

He snorted. "I'm not sure Olivia ever cared about me. Maybe she did. I don't know. Cartland, though, was rich and extravagant. I found out later he gave her things, made her a lot of empty promises about a future. She told me once she would never be poor again. We fought constantly about money, about the apartment and how it reminded her of the home she'd left, about the brand of dish detergent we bought, for Pete's sake. I tried to understand, but there was only so much I could do. We were on our own. We were young. Wealth was not an option. In the end, it didn't matter how much money we had, it was never enough." He glanced away. "Even our baby wasn't enough to keep her home."

"She was probably afraid it would all disappear one day and she'd be out on the street," Katie said.

"Yeah, I guess. Olivia is a very insecure woman. You wouldn't know it to look at her, but when you get close, you can see a very scared person in there. A long time ago, I used to feel sorry for her," he said. "Then I found out she'd used the baby to trick me into marriage, and I stopped feeling sorry for Olivia." He let out a short, angry gust. "I stopped feeling anything for her."

"How did you find out?"

He sank back onto the wood and closed his eyes. That night came flooding back, a deluge of memories that wouldn't be held back any longer. They flooded his mind, seeping into the crevices, filling every corner. He wanted to dam up the relentless pictures, but he couldn't. It was time to let them through, to deal with the past that had haunted his every move, every thought, for too long.

He swallowed, then began. "That night, Olivia went out. Again. I was fed up with her taking off and not telling me where she was going. So I went into her room—we were in separate beds by then—and started looking for some clue to where she was spending her nights. Because it certainly wasn't with me."

A light trickle of rain began, tapping softly against the wood. Matt went on, barely aware of the weather.

"I found a letter to her from Cartland. He loved her, wanted to be with her." Matt let out a chuff of disgust.

He pressed his hands to his temples, forced himself to finish. "In the letter, he talked about how he'd offered her money for an abortion." He shook his head. "I think about that sometimes, about how it would have been if she'd gone through with it, if we hadn't met…if I'd never known my son." He pinched the bridge of his nose to stop the rush of tears threatening his eyes.

Despite what had happened that night, and despite all the years since, Matt was grateful he'd had those few months with his son to carry him through the sleepless nights and anguished days that came after his child was gone.

"The letter…there was more. I should have stopped reading then. I should have shredded the damned thing before—'' Matt closed his eyes. The stark, sharp handwriting flashed in his memory, a slide show of destructive words. "Cartland," he spat out, the word a curse, "the bastard, knew when Olivia got pregnant. Recounted that night in detail, in fact. And then, oh God, it all added up. The baby hadn't been early," Matt covered his eyes with his hands, but the image of the letter was a stubborn mule, "he hadn't even been *mine.*''

"Oh, Matt.'' Katie clapped a hand over her mouth.

"*That*…that was what damned near killed me.'' His throat clogged with the hot sting of unshed tears. "I loved that baby, I loved him more than life,'' Matt said, the words now coming in a strangled whisper, "he was my son, no matter whose DNA was in him. He was *everything.*''

The rain began to fall in earnest now, fat drops plopping onto the wood and grass. Thunder rumbled in the distance, the wind whistling its accompaniment.

"And then he died. He…he was only three months old.'' His voice broke, along with his control, and his tears mingled with the rain.

"Matt.'' Katie reached for him, drawing him into her arms, pulling his head to her chest. He remained rigid for a second, then relaxed, sinking into the comfort of Katie.

The dam against his grief shattered. Matt didn't try to hold it back. Not anymore. He needed to mourn the baby he'd lost, the hope, the promise that had all died in the back bedroom of a tiny walk-up apartment.

"I loved him so much,'' he whispered hoarsely. "When I found him that night, he was so still, so quiet. On his stomach, not on his back. I hadn't been able to bear his crying and just laid him down like that because he liked to sleep that way. Any other night, I would have gone in after he was asleep and rolled him back, just in case the blanket got caught under his chin or he…I was always worried. But that night…If I'd just checked on him one more time, maybe—'' God, how he'd tortured himself with the what-ifs, the retracing of steps that could not be undone. "I picked him up, held him. But there was nothing. No breath, no sound. I tried CPR. I tried everything. But he, he…wouldn't wake up. He was so blue, so cold. It was SIDS, the hospital said, like that explained everything. But it didn't. It didn't explain a damned thing."

"Matt," Katie whispered, cradling him, soothing him.

But the guilt and the anguish were ripping him apart, a shredder in his soul. He jerked away from Katie and got to his feet. "It was my fault, don't you see? I didn't watch him that night. I wasn't *there* when my son died. I wasn't there when he needed me…I was—" He tried to finish it, to let the last of the truth come out. But he couldn't.

If he told Katie that he'd been a raving, bitter drunk, incapable of seeing anything but those horrible, devastating words, if he told her he'd been too focused on his own rage and betrayal to see anything at all, she'd be gone faster than he could take a breath.

"It wasn't your fault, Matt, it was a tragedy. That's all." She went to his side, brought her face to his and laid a soft kiss on his lips. Again and again, she kissed him, offering solace, forgiveness.

Guilt clawed at him, but his own selfish need for Katie overrode it all. Just for tonight, he'd pretend he wasn't the man he was and let that look remain in Katie's eyes a little longer. Capture one more moment of perfection before it all went away again.

Talking about his son's death was like losing him all over again. He couldn't take losing Katie tonight, too.

"*Katie.* Oh God, Katie, I need you." The rain sheeted down on them, plastering her hair against her face, mingling with his tears.

Chapter Eleven

Katie had never intended to fall in love with Matt Webster, but she had. Like Alice down the rabbit hole, there had been little chance of turning around and pretending he'd never happened. She wanted nothing more than to wrap her body and her heart around him. And oh, how Matt Webster needed someone to do that.

When the rain let loose, they dashed into the barn. Matt kicked the door shut, then stood there, shirt bonded to his chest, hair slick against his head. Vulnerability and uncertainty hovered around him.

She didn't hesitate. She crossed to him, twined her fingers with his. "Matt, you're a good man. What happened wasn't—"

"Shh." He shook his head, his eyes closed as if he couldn't bear to hear her finish. "Don't say it. Don't say anything."

His hands moved to her waist and tightened around her. Then he kissed her, claiming her mouth with a ferocity she'd never felt before. It was as primitive as the pounding storm outside. She was lost, like a sailboat buffeted by a tempest.

She'd come here to offer him comfort. But there was no comfort in this kiss. Only a powerful, electric connection of wanting. His hands roamed her back, traveled down and over her buttocks, shifting the silky material of her dress. Nerves tingled, screamed with desire at every juncture. The wet fabric was slippery, sensual.

Katie's breathing ratcheted up, immediately coming hard, fast. She was blinded by the feelings that bombarded her, seeking only to know more. She explored the ridges and planes of his body through the thin, soaked fabric of his shirt, touching his chest, sliding down his back and then up to his shoulders, over the valleys and hard, tight muscles of Matt's torso.

His erection pressed against her, pulsing his need, inflaming her own. The damp fabric between them might as well have been invisible. Its slippery wetness only magnified their closeness.

He was everything she had denied herself. The deprivation amplified when he took her lower lip with his teeth in teasing nips. She groaned, pressed harder, tugged at his shirt, wanting, needing, not even able to voice the powerful rush that roared through her.

She yanked at his shirt, nearly ripping off the buttons in agonizing need to have more to touch. Between them, his nimble fingers undid the tiny buttons, knuckles brushing against her breasts. Panting, her vision blurred, Katie jerked his shirt off and tossed it to the floor.

"Katie," Matt growled. He lifted her off the ground and hoisted her onto the table. Instinctively, she wrapped her legs around his waist, pinning him against her. Pulse met pulse, hearts beating the same staccato rhythm.

"Matt." The word came out in a moan. She pulled back,

tried to form coherent thoughts. "I want…" She hesitated, unsure of saying the words she'd never uttered. It was taking a chance of monumental proportions, a step forward into territory she'd never explored.

Matt wasn't Steve. She wasn't the girl she'd been a year ago. She loved Matt, loved him with a depth that extended far beyond today.

Right now, she wanted nothing more than to offer herself to him. Out of love. The way it should be, the way she'd dreamed it would be for her one day. Katie reached out and stroked a hand along his chest, feeling the warmth of his skin against her palm. The fear of failure, of rejection, dissipated. "Make love to me."

"Oh, Katie." Fire lit his eyes and he crushed her closer. Ravenously, he devoured her mouth, capturing her heart and soul with burning touches.

He reached for the zipper behind her and tugged it down, exposing her upper body to his gaze. She felt the rush of cool air against her skin and her nipples puckered tightly under the soft satin of her bra. There were no thoughts in Katie's head, only the fire-red flood of desire.

He cupped her breasts through the material, caressing the tips with his fingers. "Matt…Matt," she repeated his name, unable to put into words the incredible feelings rushing through her.

She wanted to scream at him to hurry, to slow down. To do anything. He smiled and slid a finger down the center of her upper body. "Perfect," he whispered, lowering his mouth to hers again.

She moaned and cupped his head, arching against him. He pulled away, his mouth hovering over hers. He was breathing hard and his voice was thick, deep. "Before we go any farther, I need to be the voice of reason. I've got about five seconds of lucidity here," he brushed his mouth

against hers, "because you're making it damned impossible
to think."

"I'm sorry." But she wasn't at all.

"I bet you are," he said, grinning. "Seriously, Katie, are
you sure? About making love? Because if we keep this up,"
he nibbled along her neck, inhaling her skin, "there'll be
no going back very soon."

"I've never been surer of anything in my life." She
tipped her head back, allowing him greater access. "I
want…I want my first time to be with you."

He jerked back. "First time? What do you—" He cut the
sentence short when the answer became obvious. "Oh my
God, Katie, why didn't you tell me?"

"I just did."

"Yeah, but…" He took two steps away. "I can't…we
shouldn't.… Why didn't you say anything?"

She looked away. "I didn't think you'd want me if you
knew I was, well, inexperienced."

He approached again, cradled her chin, and turned her to
look at him. "Want you? Katie, I've never wanted anyone
more in my life." He drew his thumb along the line of her
lower lip and Katie nearly cried with craving him again.
"Honey, why would you think that?"

"Steve said I was…frigid."

He laughed aloud. "You, my darling, are anything but
frigid. You're the hottest, sexiest woman I know."

"Then why won't you make love to me?"

"I want to. I think that's obvious." He chuckled.
"But—" He made a sweeping gesture at the barn. "This
isn't exactly a romantic spot. Nor is it the kind of place or
experience you should have. Your first time should be special," he laughed, "and comfortable."

"This is special," she said, trying to draw him back. Everything in her screamed to continue, to toss the brakes he kept trying to apply right out the window.

Matt saw the wanting written all over her face. If he were a lesser man, he could have easily taken advantage of the situation and whisked Katie off to a pile of hay somewhere. A few months ago, hell, a few weeks ago, he had been that man. But meeting her had somehow changed all that for him.

Her eyes were clear, free of guile and deceit. Lord, who knew there were women like her? And what had he done to have her walk into his life at the precise time when he needed to believe again in truth?

"Katie, you deserve much better than this. You should be in a five-star hotel, surrounded by silk, flowers—"

She stepped forward and placed a finger on his lips. "Shh. Stop telling me what I need. I'm a big girl, in case you hadn't noticed, and what I need right now is you."

Yearning exploded within him. He hauled her against him, feeling a sudden, fierce need to hold her close. She wrapped her hands around his back. The warmth of her pressed against his chest.

"Katie," he murmured, "what are you doing to me?"

"No more than you're doing to me." Her voice was shaky.

"I can't think straight when I'm around you."

"Are you saying I'm driving you crazy?"

"You're pushing me right over the edge."

"Gee, you really know how to flatter a girl." She wrapped her arms around his neck, pulling his head closer, within nibbling distance of those magnificent breasts. "Let me see how far it is to the edge."

"I meant...I wanted to say," he stumbled, his eyes and his mind entirely on the sweet curve of her breasts. The words he wanted to say were dancing in the back of his head, out of reach. The last time he'd felt flustered around a girl he'd been twelve. He'd asked Mary Lou Hennessey from down the street to ride double on his bike. She'd turned him down flat when she'd gotten a look at the thin handlebars that would be her mode of transportation.

This time was different. He was a grown man and Katie was a grown woman. He wasn't asking her to ride double to the Dairy Queen with him; he just wanted her to know that meeting her had changed something in him. And it was coming out all wrong.

He hauled himself up to meet her gaze. "I meant that you are the most unforgettable woman I have ever met." He tilted her chin up and kept his eyes on hers, depths of un-cooled passion still reflected in their azure depths.

She turned a pretty shade of pink. "I doubt you've met many ladies in banana suits."

"No, I can't say that I have." He traced along her jaw with his thumb. "I don't expect I ever will again."

There was more in his words than he was willing to say. More meaning, more tenderness, more emotion. He stared at her, letting his gaze caress her peach-soft skin, allowing his eyes to do what he dared not do with his hands.

He had the funny feeling that if he *really* touched Katie right now, if he made love to her, it would be the kind of experience that would rock his soul.

He had wanted women before. He had felt lust before. But he had never needed a woman as badly as he did Katie. She filled a gap in him, like insulation in a wall, warming him and melting the icy layers around his heart and soul, opening him up again to the world. That feeling—a deep-seated need—scared the hell out of him. It was the same feeling that had overwhelmed him on the dance floor. Then, and now, he couldn't get past his own fear.

He shook his head, stepped away. A draft filled the space

where he'd been. "I'm not the man for you. I wish I were. But I'm not. Later, you'll see—"

"I love you, Matt."

He jerked to attention. Had he heard her right? She loved him? Katie was handing him the most incredible gift he could imagine, no strings attached. But she'd done that knowing only half the story about him. It would be cruel to let her hope that he could be anything beyond what he was—a man with a horrible past who wasn't capable of the kind of future she deserved. Katie Dole was so clearly the kind of woman who wanted a husband, a father to her future children. Not a man so selfish he couldn't even be trusted to watch his own child.

It would be so easy to lie, to say the words she wanted to hear, and then slip into her arms and take her to his bed. With regret, he shook his head again.

"You love who you think I am, Katie."

"You're wrong."

His smile hurt his cheeks. "I wish I were." He slid her dress back up her shoulders. The rain had stopped and the tentative chirps of birds came from the trees. "I'm sorry."

She looked confused, hurt. He wanted so badly to erase those emotions from her face. "Was it something I said? Did? I know I'm not very good at this, and—"

"*You* are perfect. It's me who needs a little...renovation. Actually, a lot." She sat there, hair in disarray, lips swollen and all he wanted to do was find the nearest blanket and flat surface.

He clenched his fists at his side and willed himself to think of anything but sex. Snow, Santa Claus, television remote controls, table linens—no, too close to blankets. He picked up his shirt off the floor and slipped it on. The fabric was cold and wet, the perfect shocker for an over-heated mind.

Katie stilled his hands with her own. "Matt, wait. Let me tell you something first." She hesitated, then went on. "A year ago, I made a huge mistake by being blind to the truth. I'm not going to do that again, only seeing what I want to because I don't like the reality." She smiled at him and he found himself wanting her all over again. "You taught me that it's okay to take a risk, to tango across the floor and stumble once in a while. To tell a man I love him and not expect anything in return."

"Katie, I'm sorry—"

"No, it's okay."

"It's not. You deserve more than I can offer." He sighed. "There are things about me you don't know."

"Then tell me. Trust me."

"I can't. Not now. Maybe never." He wanted to lift this heavy weight off his chest and toss it away. To free himself from the guilt that hung over everything he did. But he couldn't. If there was one thing he couldn't bear right now, it would be to see scorn and recrimination in Katie's gaze. To have her hate him for being a selfish, irresponsible drunk.

"I can't," he repeated.

She cupped his face. "Deception does nothing but eat away at everything that's good. You get all wrapped up in the illusion because admitting the truth forces you out of your comfort zone. Trust me, I know this."

"Katie—"

"No, hear me out. I love you, Matt. A year ago, I couldn't have said that without being certain you felt the same. Comfort zone." She reached behind herself and pulled up her zipper, then hopped off the table. "Well, I'm tired of living that way. I'm changing lanes," she smiled at the pun, "and if you're not ready to do that yet, it's all right. I'm okay either way."

He thought about what she'd said, about moving past the

crater he'd been in for eleven years. About not letting a sin of omission, a fear of confessing, keep his life from continuing. "You're right." He sighed. "But there are some things you can't forget. Mistakes other people won't forgive."

"Whatever role you think you played in losing your son may not be the whole picture at all." She laid a hand on his shoulder. "Did you ever think you might be taking the blame for something that wasn't entirely your fault?"

He looked past her, at the walls that were as decrepit as his own life. "You don't know what you're talking about."

"Maybe I don't. But until you're ready to face everything, you won't either." She let go and moved away. She blinked and he saw the glimmer of tears in her eyes. "I have a life to live. I'd love it if you were a part of it. But only if you're ready to be honest with yourself and with me. I'm through pretending."

She placed a soft, chaste kiss on his lips and then walked away, leaving Matt alone in the barn with his regrets.

The numbers refused to add up. Katie could turn the adding machine upside down, even throw it against the wall, and still the red would outweigh the black.

It didn't take a CPA to see that A Pair of Posies was in serious trouble. Katie sighed. One more time, she fed in the bills and receipts. Five minutes later, she stared at the same negative number as before.

"How's it going?" Sarah placed a plate of brownies beside her. Katie sighed and replaced the adding machine with the plate, immediately launching into the chocolate.

"That bad, huh?"

"Actually, it could be worse. At least we paid the rent. We still have a roof over our heads." Katie flipped through the stack of bills on the desk in the back room. "We just can't heat it or light it or…'' she flipped some more, ''use the telephone.''

Sarah sunk into a chair. ''Oh.''

Katie dropped her head to her hands. ''We were on the brink to begin with, but when Olivia canceled those orders and the MacGilvrays called off their daughter's wedding—''

''Justifiably, though,'' Sarah said. ''When a girl finds out her fiancé is stretching the truth about being an underwear model, she's got a right to be upset.''

''I doubt she expected to see him 'modeling' for two hundred other women as a Chippendale dancer.'' Katie laughed. ''That must have been one interesting bachelorette party.''

''Think they left him a tip?''

Katie laughed again, then sobered when she saw the negative on the adding machine. ''This is my fault. I let the Olivia thing get out of hand. I never should have—''

''Stop. It's not your fault.'' Sarah hugged Katie's shoulders. ''Come on, we've been in scrapes worse than this and always—''

''I'll sell my Toyota. If I have to go anywhere, I'll just borrow the van. Or walk.''

''You love that car. Besides, the van is on its last legs. We'll be lucky to get a half dozen more deliveries out of it.''

''I love the store more.'' She swept her hand around the room. ''This is our dream, Sarah. I'm not about to let it go.''

Sarah gave her arm a little punch. ''That's the Katie I like to see.'' She sorted through the bills. ''Let's put our heads together and come up with a way to make this work.''

Forty minutes later, they didn't have much of a solution. Cutting back what little there was left to trim would help for the next month, but wouldn't pay the immediate bills.

Katie sighed and ate two more brownies. At this rate, she'd be a fat shop-owner failure.

The phone rang. Katie hurried to answer it, saying a quick prayer on the way. "A Pair of Posies."

"I'm looking for Katie Dole." The woman's voice on the other end was cultured, refined. Pleasant.

"This is her. How can I help you?"

"This is Georgianne Webster, Matt's mother. He speaks very highly of you."

"He does?"

"My son isn't so good at expressing how he feels." Georgianne laughed. "But I know, just from looking at him when he mentions your name that he cares a great deal."

"Oh." Katie resisted the urge to pump Matt's mother for more information.

"He mentioned you owned this shop. I'm hosting a dinner party later this month and would like some new arrangements. I was thinking of lilies and tulips, maybe daffodils. Real springy, happy designs." Her excited, friendly voice made it sound as if the dinner party wouldn't be complete without the shop's arrangements. "I've been using the Lawford florist for my weekly orders, but realized yours is closer. Would you be available to come see the house, maybe make some suggestions? I could use a fresh eye."

"Certainly! My partner, Sarah, is the designer, so I'll bring her along, if that's okay."

"Wonderful. Do you have time today? Or tomorrow?"

"Today is perfect." Immediately would be better, like before the bank closed, but Katie didn't say that. "How about four-thirty?" They agreed on the time and hung up. Katie flashed Sarah a thumbs-up.

"We got a job," she said. "Looks like a big one, too."

"Great! Who with?"

Katie grimaced. "Matt's mother. Think it's a pity job?"

"Who cares? It's money in the bank." Sarah took a brownie off the plate. "I don't know what's wrong with me today. I have this incredible craving for chocolate." She took a huge bite and munched for a minute.

"You never finished telling me what happened with him this afternoon. Or with Olivia." Sarah moved the plate to the other side of the table. "I'm holding these hostage until I get details."

Katie laughed. She recounted what had transpired, running through the encounter with Olivia, Miss Tanner's information and finally, her visit to Matt. "I told him when he was ready to move on with his life, I'd be here."

"Good for you! I don't think you'll have long to wait, though. That guy is crazy about you."

"I hope so." She plopped her chin into her hand. "It wasn't easy to walk away from him."

"You did the right thing."

"I know." Katie sighed. "But that doesn't keep me warm at night."

Sarah laughed. "We need to get you a cat."

"No, we need to get the Webster job." Katie shook off the blue mood that was trying to get a hold of her. There was nothing she could do about Matt, but there was plenty she could do about the store. She grabbed a notepad from the desk. "Let's run down some ideas for spring arrangements."

For the next hour, they brainstormed. At four, they climbed into the van and headed to the Webster house. "I can't believe Jack went to that disaster training class for the police department." Sarah spread a thick blanket over the worn bench seat and stuffed a pillow behind her back. "He should be here, waiting on me hand and foot."

"He'll be back on Friday. You're not even due until next Monday."

"I don't think this—" Sarah let out an *oomph* and rubbed her stomach where the baby had kicked, "—little football player wants to wait that long."

Their eighteen-year-old A Pair of Posies van wheezed and shook the entire way to the Webster house, located on the outskirts of town, a few miles past the Emery farm. Katie was looking forward to Georgianne's order but dreaded the possibility of running into Matt. She'd walked away, resolved to wait for him, but knew she'd melt if he even glanced her way.

When they pulled up in front of the imposing Webster house, Katie had to fight the urge to gape. Not house— mansion—that was the only way to describe it. She'd never seen it up close, had only caught glimpses of it between the trees and seven-foot wrought-iron gate that guarded it from the outside world. There had to be at least thirty rooms in the sprawling white residence, all with large windows fronting the expansive property. It was impeccably landscaped with graceful roses and animal-shaped shrubs that formed a welcoming parade along the drive. Money practically hung from every leaf, every petal.

"Wow," Sarah said.

"My thoughts exactly." Katie shut off the van, took a deep breath and flashed a semi-confident smile at Sarah. "We're up to this job. We're ready for the big time. Right?"

"You betcha." But even Sarah looked taken aback by the imposing house.

They got out of the van, made their way up granite steps and rang the bell. A melody softly pealed inside.

The door opened and an elegant woman who could only be Georgianne Webster smiled at Katie and clasped both her hands. "Katie, how nice to meet you."

Matt's mother was clad in a soft gray silk pantsuit, her

ash-blond hair pulled back from her face with a clip. The youthful style somehow fitted her. She had to be at least fifty years old, but had the flawless face of a younger woman. She greeted Sarah, then invited them inside.

Katie crossed the threshold into a magnificent home that could mean thousands of dollars of business for the store over the next year. The foyer had a marble floor and a Chippendale settee flanked by a bombé chest. Around the corner, she glimpsed two seating arrangements in the living room, where a pair of antique chairs was grouped below the window, looking out over a magnificent view of woods and gardens.

Katie should have been impressed, awed. Instead, she had to force herself not to look for Matt among the impeccable antiques and exquisite artwork.

It would take one hell of a lot of nails and hammering to work Katie's exit out of his system. Unfortunately, that job required more nails than Matt had on hand.

After she'd left, he'd set to work building a wall, heaving and shoving the wood into place by himself, ignoring the tearing pain in his back and the sweat pouring down his face. As he sawed and hammered, he worked through a gamut of emotions, starting with frustration and ending with idiocy.

How could he have let her walk away? She was right. Delaying the truth was stupid. It was like putting a Band-Aid over a broken bone. It didn't help, and even worse, barely masked the real problem.

Once this last wall was in place—if he didn't finish this one, all his work on the other three would fall apart—he was going to run home, change and find her. Tell her the whole truth and let the chips fall where they may.

There. A room. A few two-by-fours, erected in squares,

then hammered into place. It didn't look like much until it was paired with another section, then a third and finally, a fourth, creating a tangible space. His new beginning was starting to feel real, concrete.

Matt took a step back, admiring the work he'd accomplished. A week ago, there'd been nothing here. Now, there was a skeleton. He unstrapped the heavy leather belt and laid it on top of his toolbox. In the cooler, a bottle of water remained from his lunch. He twisted off the top and tipped it into his mouth.

The musical call of alcohol played softly in the back of his mind. It probably always would. The song didn't sound as loud or insistent as it used to, which he supposed was a very good thing.

Over the bottom edge of the bottle, he saw a flash of blond hair. Matt lowered the water, recapped it, returned it to the cooler, and waited for his ex-wife to reach him. At the rate Olivia was marching across the field, it didn't take her long, even in heels.

"Well, hello, Olivia, what a surprise," he said dryly.

"What are you doing here?" She never had bothered with niceties.

"I live here. Or rather, I will, once I finish."

"Don't toy with me, Matthew. I want to know why you're in Mercy, destroying my life."

"I didn't come back to get revenge or make you suffer." He shook his head. "It's always been about you, hasn't it? About how Olivia is affected. Did you ever think I might be back for me? For my own life?"

"People are talking, Matthew."

He shrugged. "Let them."

"They're talking about that night. About how you—"

"Like I said, let them talk. I don't have anything to hide. Not anymore." He brushed some sawdust from his pants.

"Why does it bother you? You're the innocent party, as far as everyone knows."

"You've…never told? Anyone?"

"No. No one until Katie, and even she doesn't know everything. That's one burden I shouldered all by myself." He let out a sigh. "I can't do that anymore. It's time to move on past this ghost of a life I've been living."

Olivia snorted. "With Katie?"

"Maybe. I hope so." Matt took a seat on the toolbox. "What about you, Olivia? Have you moved on? Or have you done what I did and let the secrets and the lies multiply until you've forgotten where the truth is buried?"

She didn't answer. Instead, she squinted against the sun and looked past him, at the acreage beyond the house.

"I'm done with that. I don't care what people think about me anymore or what the truth will do to their feelings." He got to his feet and crossed to the wall he'd just built. The posts felt sturdy, solid. Nearly permanent. "Working out here, with nothing but the birds and deer to keep me company, gave me a lot of time to think.

"Two hours ago, I pushed away the first woman I've truly cared about, hell, loved," and with that, a slow smile stole across his face as he realized, yes, he did truly, deeply love Katie, and the joy of it burst in his heart, "because I didn't want to tell her the truth. I didn't want to face what kind of man I'd been in the past. I didn't want to lose her. But by keeping that secret, I lost her anyway." He snorted. "Ironic, isn't it?"

When she spoke, her voice was soft, almost sad. "I have more at stake than you. My name. My business."

"Doesn't all of it feel empty when you keep a secret? When you have to produce lie after lie to keep everything intact, like a juggler with glass balls?"

Her face tightened. "It will destroy everything."

"Come on, Olivia. It's been eleven years since Matthew died." She flinched when he said their son's name. "Why not get it all out? Set the truth free."

She spun to face him. "Because it's better if it just stays buried. Period. Don't go digging up graves, Matt."

"*Why?*" He leaned in, searching her icy-blue eyes. "Is there something you're hiding in that grave?"

Olivia's hand whipped out and slapped him across the face. The sound echoed in the stillness. A sharp sting radiated across his jaw. Before she could do it again, Matt grabbed her wrist, controlling the primal urge to strike back. "You *do* have something to hide, don't you? Well, I'm not paying for your lies anymore." He flung her hand away, picked up his tools and walked away.

"Matthew." Her voice cracked on the last syllable.

"What?" He turned around to face her. Maybe it was just a trick of the light, but Matt could swear he saw a sheen of tears in Olivia's eyes.

She let out a breath. Her shoulders seemed to sag. "We almost had something here, didn't we?"

He swallowed. "Yeah, we did."

"I'm sorry," she said softly.

"Me, too." His sigh was heavy. "Me, too."

She nodded once, then strode away, retracing her path to her car with the same speedy pace as before.

Chapter Twelve

As soon as Olivia left, Matt followed his hunches. Too many puzzle pieces had been scattered by Miss Tanner's conversation with Katie and Olivia's reluctance to speak about losing the baby. He made a stop at the county coroner's office—and found exactly what he now expected to find. The words on the report didn't instantly absolve Matt's guilt, but they did explain a few of the missing holes in the story.

Matt sped back to his parent's house, urging the bike to hurry. The storm had left the air smelling fresh, clean. New. To Matt, it seemed an apt setting for a man about to wipe his own slate clean.

He skidded to a halt when he saw the A Pair of Posies van parked in the driveway. Katie.

He leapt off the bike, took one step toward the door, then turned and caught the heavy motorcycle before it crashed to the ground. *Kickstand, idiot.* He laughed at himself, then flicked the kickstand and set the bike.

He ran up the stairs and burst through the door. No one

was in the hallway. What did he expect? She'd be waiting by the door?

His shoes clattered on the floor as Matt checked room after room for Katie. And then, through the windowpane in the dining room, he saw her. Katie, framed by flowers, exiting the greenhouse beside his mother and Sarah. She had a rose in her hand, and sniffed the petals once while she talked. Her face was animated, lively. Happy.

She had her hair swept up, exposing the same curve of neck he'd been nibbling on just hours ago. She'd changed into the dress she'd worn the night he met her in the Corner Pocket. He didn't know if she had purposely picked that outfit, but just the thought that she might have had him in mind when she pulled it out of the closet pleased him.

The sweet, lilting sound of her laughter carried on the spring air and into the house. How he craved that sound, needed to hear it. At least once a day, for the next, oh, one hundred years.

Matt knew the back door opened into the kitchen, so he headed there. He skidded to a halt on the ceramic tile.

"Have you been working in this rain, Matthew?" His father stood by the refrigerator, the door open. Light and cold air spilled across the floor.

For once, his father didn't seem to have any hidden meanings in his question. A simple conversation. That was something the two of them rarely had.

"Some. It didn't rain long." Matt peered past his father. Katie was just coming up the walk. "I got some walls up, though."

"Good. Glad to hear it." He shut the door and Matt saw his father was holding a half eaten salami sandwich.

"Mom's on her way in," Matt said.

Edward gave a guilty start, then tossed the remains of his snack into the trash. "I was, ah…looking for an…apple."

The snippet of humanness in his father was another surprise. Imagine that, Edward Webster sneaking unhealthy food behind his wife's back, then disposing of the evidence. "I won't tell." Matt smiled. "As long as you take better care of yourself."

His father's lips curved up, slowly, as if he were using his smile for the first time. "I'll do that. Just don't bring home any more salami, okay?"

"Deal." The back door opened and the three women entered. None of them saw Matt right away. They were engrossed in a conversation about flowers, clearly a common link.

"Sarah, the rest room is right at the end of the hall. When you're through, take a moment to look at the wallpaper in the dining room. I love your design idea and think with the right colors, it would be the perfect—" She stopped, finally noticing the men in her kitchen. "Matthew! You're all…dirty."

"I've been working off some frustration." His gaze never left Katie's. She didn't say a word, just clutched the rose.

"You really should take a shower, dear. You're tracking dirt all over—"

"I don't think I can wait that long to say what I need to say," he told his mother. But his gaze never left Katie's.

"I apologize, but I can't wait at all," Sarah said with a laugh. She grimaced, then headed toward the door that led to the hall. "I've got someone here who insists I find the rest room."

Katie didn't notice Sarah leave. She was aware of nothing but Matt. Like radar, her whole body was attuned to him.

When she'd entered the kitchen and seen him, she'd felt a powerful rush of joy. That was love, she knew. Twenty years from now, she knew that rush would come back whenever he pulled in the driveway or entered a room.

If they were still together. After this afternoon, she wasn't so sure that was a possibility.

"I meant to take a shower before I came to see you," Matt said. "I wanted to come to you clean at least." He smiled.

When he did, the room, the other people around them, dropped away. The air was laden with unfinished business between them. Matt was watching her intently, sapphire eyes full of desire, full of something more. She felt heat rise to her face.

He had made it clear he wasn't ready to move on or to tackle anything more serious. And yet, here he was, standing across from her and watching her every move. Like a man in love. Which, of course, he wasn't. He was just pretending. Putting on a show for his parents, just as he did at the wedding. Wasn't he?

"I don't mind the dirt," she said. In fact, his disarray was sexy, more masculine than a tuxedo or business suit. She had to resist the urge to reach out and whisk the sawdust from his hair.

"Good. Because I have something to tell you. To tell all of you," he said, his gaze taking in his parents, too, "and if I wait any longer, I think I'll go insane. Please, sit down."

Georgianne took a seat at one end of the kitchen table, Edward the other. Katie sat in the seat across from Matt. From the front of the house, the doorbell rang. Everyone ignored it. Whoever it was could come back later.

Matt folded his hands before him, steepling his fingers against his forehead. She saw a wave of mental resolve harden in his face and he laid his hands flat against the wood. "There's something about the night the baby died that I didn't tell you. I figured you'd disown me. Hell, I wouldn't blame you if you still did."

"Matt, we'd never—" his mother began.

Matt shook his head. "Don't. Wait until I've said what I need to before you make promises you can't keep." He swallowed, then began. "The baby's death was my fault."

Georgianne gasped. Edward sat stone-still. The doorbell rang again, and once more, no one moved. Katie realized Matt was laying the blame squarely at his own feet, even after what she'd told him about Miss Tanner. It would be easy to point the finger elsewhere, to stop the rumors by blaming another. But he didn't.

He seemed to pull on some well of strength within him before continuing. "I was drinking that night. I'd found something that…upset me. I don't want to get into what it was. Olivia has suffered enough and the ending of our marriage had started long before. I ignored all our problems, thinking it would work out. I was blind, but that night, I saw everything." He ran a hand through his hair. Motes of sawdust floated to the floor.

"I drank myself into oblivion. I think I passed out, maybe fell asleep. I don't know. I don't remember. When my son stopped breathing," he swallowed, then dragged the words out, one painful one after the other, "I was stone drunk on the kitchen floor, curled up with a bottle and my own sorry self."

"Matthew," his mother said, reaching for him.

He shook his head and pushed her hand away. "When I came to, the baby was dead. I was too late. Too damned *late*." His eyes were misting, his knuckles white. "I'm an alcoholic. A decade ago, I had my last drink. But back then, when it mattered, I was a stupid, selfish drunk. And because of that, I lost the only thing that ever mattered to me." His gaze focused on Katie. "When I tried to keep my own guilt hidden, I lost the only woman I ever loved."

"It wasn't your fault, Matt," Olivia said.

Everyone turned. She stood in the doorway, her face a

mess. Black smudges ringed her eyes and there were clear blotches where her makeup was entirely gone. "I came here to stop you from telling them what happened."

She shook her head. "I guess I underestimated you. I thought you'd tell them about Jacob. About what I did." Her voice broke and the tears began again, a slow trickling break in the steel composure of Olivia. She glanced at Georgianne apologetically. "When no one answered the door, I let myself in. I'd seen Matt's bike and Katie's van, and figured he was in here, telling you what a horrible person I am." She bit her lip. "But you didn't, did you, Matt?"

He shook his head.

She smiled a little, then her gaze dropped to the floor. "I guess I never really knew what a good guy you were. I saw you as a meal ticket."

"Olivia," Matt said, waiting until she looked at him to continue. "You were seventeen and pregnant. Desperate. I understand that now. I don't blame you. You gave me the greatest gift of my life. Matthew was the best—"

"Please don't say it. Please don't talk about him. I can't—" She ran a hand through her hair, displacing the carefully-done tendrils. "I tried to make it work between us, Matt, I really did. But I just couldn't do it. The baby—"

"That baby had a name, Olivia," Matt cut in. "Why didn't you *ever* call him by name?"

"Because then I would have loved him too much." She sank against the wall, looking broken, defeated. "I couldn't do that, I couldn't call him by name when I knew…" tears began to stream down her face, "…when I knew he was going to die."

Silence blanketed the room as Olivia's words sank in among the stunned people at the table.

"What are you talking about?" Edward demanded.

Olivia turned to look at Matt and for the first time, he

saw the reflection of his own grief, his own guilt, in her eyes. Olivia had suffered just as much as he had, but she had covered it all with a mask of haughty indifference. He hadn't been the only one who hurt, who went to bed with an aching heart every single night for eleven years.

"It was my fault, Matt," she continued. "I'm so sorry I didn't tell you. I meant to, but then…you were gone."

"What are you talking about?" Edward asked.

"The baby didn't die of SIDS, like I told everyone." Olivia took a deep breath. "He had a heart condition called hypertrophic cardiomyopathy. It was genetic. My brother and my Aunt Colleen's baby had it." She looked at Matt. "I should have—"

"Olivia, I know. I saw the autopsy report today."

She blinked. "You did?"

"I'd put the pieces together, with a little help." He cast a quick glance at Katie. "So I stopped off at the county coroner's office today and got a copy." He pulled the sheets out of his back pocket and handed them to her.

She took a cursory glance at it, but it was clear she'd read the words before. "Then why…why didn't you tell everyone it was really my fault?"

"Olivia, it was still just as much mine. If I'd been sober, maybe I would have heard or seen Matthew stop breathing. I could have gotten him to the hospital in time. Maybe. Maybe not." He let out a long sigh. "Either way, I think we've both suffered enough. Don't you?"

A tear slipped down her face. "I lied to the doctors, Matt. I didn't tell them about my family history. I…I thought maybe our baby would be different. I mean, I didn't have it, so maybe my children wouldn't either. I was young and I guess I thought if I didn't say anything about the disease, it couldn't happen."

"You could have told me, Olivia." Matt's voice broke.

"I know." The tears were coming earnestly now, washing the rest of the makeup off her face, stripping her bare. "I was wrong. I never expected you to be a real father. I thought you'd marry me and leave me, like everyone else always had. But when you didn't, I kept hoping that it would all work out somehow."

"You kept this to yourself? All these years?" Edward asked.

She nodded, her eyes downcast, apparently unable to look at the in-laws and the husband she had deceived. "Don't you understand? It was my fault, Matt. I gave him that disease." She lowered her head to her hands and sobbed, her shoulders shaking. "I couldn't stay in that apartment, night after night, and hear him cry. Every time I heard him cry, I was afraid. I thought maybe it meant he was sick. I couldn't face it. I...I was seventeen. I know that's not an excuse, but...it was just all so overwhelming and you seemed to handle him so much better. I felt like such a failure, Matt. I couldn't face that. Or face you. And when he died—" Her voice tore on the last word.

Matt pushed his chair back and did something he should have done a long time ago. He crossed to Olivia, gently tugged her to her feet and pulled her into his arms. She sobbed against his shoulder, repeating over and over again that she was sorry. He stroked her hair, whispering to her that it was okay.

Finally forgiving her.

"Katie!" Sarah's urgent whisper came from the dining-room door. *"Katie!"*

Katie slipped over to the doorway. "What?"

Sarah motioned for her to come out into the hall. When the door swung shut behind them, Sarah held up one finger and braced her hand against the wall. She was panting hard. "I need to go to the hospital," she said between breaths.

"Now?!"

"I don't think Little Jack wants to wait any longer. My water broke in the bathroom and—" Her face contorted with pain. "*Now,* Katie," she said through gritted teeth.

"But what about Jack?"

"He'll never make it in time. I called his cell phone and told him to meet us at the hospital."

"We should call an ambulance," Katie said.

Sarah shook her head. "You know Mercy doesn't have an ambulance and the, the…" she paused to pant, "the Lawford one would take at least…twenty minutes to get here. We could be…at the hospital by then."

"Okay, okay," Katie said. "Stay right there. Let me grab my purse and I'll take you right now."

Katie turned and dashed back into the room. Olivia had sat down and was drying her eyes with a handkerchief. Georgianne and Edward both looked shell-shocked. Matt was standing by Katie's chair, a worried expression on his face. "Is Sarah all right?"

Katie shook her head and grabbed her purse off the counter. "No. She needs to get to the hospital. She's having the baby."

"Now?"

"Yup." Katie rooted around in her bag until she found the keys to the van. "I'm sorry, Matt, but I have to go." She turned to Georgianne. "Thank you, Mrs. Webster, but I really have to leave. I'll get back to you about the flowers."

"No rush, dear." Georgianne laughed. "No rush at all."

"I'm going with you," Matt said.

She paused long enough to look at him. "You don't have to. I'd understand if it might be difficult for you because—"

"I want to go with you," he said. "I'll drive. You help Sarah."

"Okay." She and Matt started for the doorway.

"Son, before you go..."

Matt pivoted, his hand still holding the swinging door open. "What?"

"There's something I need to say to you. I was too damned stubborn to say it before." Edward raised himself up on his arms, slowly got out of his chair and crossed the room to Matt. He hesitated for a second, then opened his arms. "I'm sorry, Matt. For so many things."

Matt heard the regret and vulnerability in his father's words and felt his throat constrict. His father's arms went around him and for a moment, he wasn't sure how to respond.

He hadn't felt the need or desire to hug his father since he was a boy. Not since he'd won his first baseball game at the age of seven. He'd run up to his father, arms outstretched, the joy of victory filling his young-boy heart. All he'd received in return was a stiff, one-armed pat and an admonishment to behave with more decorum in public. That cold response had hurt for a long, long time.

But that was the past. There had been a lot of new beginnings in this room tonight, Matt realized. And he would be a fool to let the wounds of the past keep him from healing the present.

He let go of the door and held on to his father. Matt wasn't sure, but he thought he felt a tear trickle onto his neck. He gripped his father harder and was rewarded with a firm bear hug in return.

"*Katie!!*" Sarah's shriek was urgent. "We have to go now!"

His father released him. "We'll talk later." Edward put an aged, wrinkled hand to Matt's cheek. "Find your hap-

piness wherever you need to, Matt. I guess I've finally realized it's your life to live, not mine.''

"Thanks, Dad.'' Matt didn't have time to let his father's
words sink in. Sarah let out a scream and he was out the
door in a flash.

"We're not going to make it,'' Katie called to Matt. She
was in the back of the van with Sarah, holding her hand and
helping her breathe. Katie's sole knowledge of childbirth
came from watching *ER,* so she wasn't even sure she was
coaching Sarah correctly.

"This baby wants out and he wants out now,'' Sarah
cried, panting hard. She squeezed Katie's hand so tightly,
Katie had to bite her lip to keep from joining in on Sarah's
screams.

"Are you sure?'' Matt glanced over the seat at them.

"Am I sure?'' Sarah gave a half laugh. "*Oh yeah.*
Please—'' pant, pant "—get me to the hospital!''

He was driving as fast as he dared in Katie and Sarah's
ramshackle van. It had been the closest vehicle to the door
and the only one big enough to let Sarah lie down on the
pillow and blanket she'd brought.

Another storm had started up almost the moment they left
the driveway. Whipping winds and driving rain were reduc-
ing visibility to almost nothing. For the tenth time that night,
Matt wished he had insisted on an ambulance instead of
thinking he could get Sarah to the hospital faster. They were
only ten minutes from the hospital now but every second
that passed increased Matt's worry.

If another baby died because of his recklessness…

"I feel the baby's head,'' Sarah screamed, all in one long
word. "He's coming *now!*''

Matt veered to the right. The rain was pouring down in
sheets. They were never going to get to the hospital in time.

Matt spotted a familiar building and gunned the engine. He drove down the bumpy road as fast as he could.

Sarah let out a loud and very unladylike curse. "What kind of road is this? The baby's going to bounce right out of—" She stopped midsentence and let out another scream.

Matt skidded to a stop and leapt out of the van. He dashed to the wide wooden doors, ignoring the rain pouring down his face, and flung them open. Then he returned to the van, turned it around and quickly backed into the barn.

The Emery farm probably wasn't the best place to have a baby but it was the closest shelter he knew of. It would have to do.

He hopped out again and pulled open the back doors to the van. Sarah had her legs propped up and was writhing with pain. "*This* is your version of a hospital?" she gasped. "Is Doctor Dolittle coming to deliver the baby?"

Despite his own fear and worry about Sarah and her child, he laughed. "It looks like the only doctor you're getting tonight is me," he told her. "And I don't talk to animals."

"What do we do?" Katie's eyes were wide, frightened.

In one vivid burst of memory, every bit of knowledge from Olivia's childbirth classes and from the delivery of his own son came hurtling back. "I need a shoelace or something to tie off the cord and some more blankets. I know the tablecloth from our breakfast is still on the table. Get that to wrap the baby in." He took in deep gulps of air, trying to think quickly. "Do you have a cell phone?"

"Sarah does. Jack got it for her in case of an emergency." Katie raced across the room to grab the cloth.

"Get it and call 9-1-1." He checked Sarah and realized they had even less time than he'd thought. "Tell them the baby is already crowning."

She tossed the tablecloth at him and hurried to the front

of the van. She was back a moment later, cell phone to her ear.

"Yes, we've done that," she said. Katie turned to Matt. "I've got the dispatcher on the line. He's going to talk us through this."

"Just get this baby out!" Sarah let out another scream. She gripped her stomach and looked down at the mound where a very determined baby resided. "Why," she gasped, "oh why, couldn't you wait till—" pant, pant "—we got to the h-h-hospital where they have d-d-drugs for this?"

"Yes, a shoelace," Katie said into the phone. She glanced around the room. Matt held out a foot to her, his hands busy helping Sarah hold her knees up.

Katie tugged off his shoe and yanked the lacing out of the holes. She dropped it next to Matt and then clambered over by Sarah's head.

"Okay, Sarah, the baby is crowning," Matt said. He wiped his palms on his pants and took a deep breath. "It's time to push."

Katie helped her friend to a half sitting position and held her while Sarah screamed and bore down, pushing the baby out. Over and over, Sarah repeated the action, as the baby worked its way into the world.

Matt's voice, so calm, so confident, helped Sarah stay focused and kept Katie from panicking. The dispatcher was reassuringly giving warnings in her ear about cleaning the baby's mouth and tying off the cord. She repeated the words to Matt. He accepted each instruction with a short nod.

Throughout it all, he never lost his cool, never showed the least bit of fear. Katie knew that if it hadn't been for him, she would have been a hysterical wreck and Sarah would have been birthing her own baby.

"The head's out!" Matt swiped inside the baby's mouth with his finger, then looked up and smiled at Sarah and

Katie. "One more push, Sarah, and we'll get the shoulders and body out."

Katie helped Sarah pull her exhausted body up one more time. Sarah gritted her teeth and moaned, putting all her effort into the push.

Matt held his hands under the baby's head, gently helping the shoulders past the birth canal. With a whoosh, a new life came sliding into the half lit interior of an aged van and a decrepit barn, right out of Sarah and into Matt's palms.

He looked down at the tiny miracle he was holding and expected to relive the pain of his son's death. But he didn't. Instead, he felt indescribable joy, soaring through his heart like an eagle in flight.

He had helped to bring a life into the world. A crying, squirming, beautiful life. He tied off the cord, wrapped the baby in the tablecloth, and handed the child to Sarah.

"It's a girl," he whispered.

Sarah burst into tears and laughter at the same time. "A girl? The way you were kicking me, I thought for sure you were a football player." She softly stroked the baby's cheek with her finger. "I'm going to name you Mattie." She looked up at Katie and Matt. "For the two people who helped you come into this world."

Katie hugged Sarah to her and marveled at the tiny infant. Then she looked at Matt and saw the awe and happiness in his eyes. Somehow, it seemed right that a new life would begin in the very place where Matt had given up on his.

The ambulance arrived a few minutes later. The paramedics loaded Sarah in, then asked Katie if she wanted to ride along. "Stay," Sarah said. "I'll be fine. Jack will be there soon. If I know him, he'll drive a hundred the whole way, lights blazing."

"Are you sure?"

"Positive. Besides, I think Matt needs you more." Sarah gave a little wave, then the paramedic shut the door.

Matt stood alone in the center of the barn. The rain pelted down on the building, coming harder now. A thunderstorm was rumbling through Mercy, with driving winds and a heavy downpour.

Once the wail of the siren began to fade, there was an uncomfortable moment of silence, punctuated only by the soft drips of water falling through the holes in the roof. And then, Matt reached for her, drawing her into the shelter of his arms, the warmth of his body. Joy soared through her.

"Katie, I'm sorry," he said, his chin against her head. "I was wrong not to tell you everything earlier." He pulled back, took in a deep gulp of air. "I wasn't sure you'd want me, after…"

"…I heard about the night your son died."

He nodded. "I was irresponsible and wrong, and—"

She put a finger to his lips. "—and very young. It wasn't your fault, Matt."

"I know that now. But for so long, Katie, I've been afraid to try again, knowing I couldn't go through that loss again. Even after I stopped drinking, I couldn't be sure of myself, couldn't trust myself to make the right choices. Then I helped Sarah have her baby and everything changed." He tipped up her chin and met her gaze. *"Everything."*

"What do you mean?"

"When the truth came out tonight and then later, when I helped deliver Sarah's baby, I realized I had finally forgiven myself. I'm ready to go forward with my life, to move on."

She had to ask, had to be sure. "With Olivia?"

"No, silly. With you." He captured her face with his hands and lowered his mouth until it was inches away from hers. "It took me a while to realize just how much I needed you. And wanted you."

"I don't think wanting was ever the problem." She grinned.

"I guess I always made myself pretty clear in that area." His expression turned serious. "What I didn't realize until tonight, until it was almost too late and I was afraid I'd lost you…" he let his voice trail off.

His breath was warm on her face, his lips so close that she knew all it would take was a slight sway in his direction to bring her mouth to his. But she stayed where she was, captivated, eager for him to finish the sentence.

He hesitated, searched her gaze. "I didn't lose you, did I?"

She shook her head. "No, Matt, not even close."

"Well, I'll just have to make sure there's no possibility of losing you in the future, then. Because I don't know what I'd do without you, Katie. I love you."

A rush of happiness ran through her, tingling all the way down. He loved her. For real. *He loves me,* she thought again. And again.

"I love you, too," she whispered, reveling in the words, pulling him closer.

And when she kissed him, with love and trust and a promise of forever in her eyes, Matt felt the crevices of pain in his heart begin to heal. He wrapped his arms around her, intertwining himself with her until he couldn't tell where he ended and she began.

He was finally home.

Epilogue

"Katie!" Matt called for his wife. The house he and his crew, with some help from his father, had finished building a year ago on the old foundation was spacious, with enough room for them and an enormous, goofy dog—the first one he'd ever had.

Katie had hung up her banana suit for good after she and Sarah had relocated A Pair of Posies to the remodeled barn, switching their business focus to floral design. His mother, thrilled with her new daughter-in-law's talent, had made sure they were the most in-demand florists in Southeastern Indiana. Olivia's business was also doing well and she sent as many clients to Katie and Sarah as they did to her. Funny how all their dreams had come true once they'd grown up and stopped living in the past.

There was a playpen in the shop for Mattie, who was now a little over a year and inquisitive as a cat. Beside the playpen, a pair of baby swings sat empty and waiting. It wouldn't be long now until the sound of crying and cooing filled both the house and the barn, Matt thought.

The house, designed by both of them, was large but not so big that he and Katie needed an intercom system to communicate. He liked being close to his wife, especially now, when he could barely let her out of his sight.

"Katie! Come here, you have to see this!" He pushed on the swinging door that led from the family room into the kitchen. Katie had her back to him. She was facing the countertop, probably still engrossed in the loaf of bread she was making. "Your brother Mark is on the Lawford Ten-Spot News." He strode over to where she was. "You'll never believe it—"

She turned around slowly. Her hands were covered in bread dough and her apron was coated with a fine sheen of flour. She opened her mouth to say something, then shut it again. Her face contorted in pain. "Matt..." She gasped. She braced her hands against the counter and then tried again. "Matt, I hope you have a good memory."

"What are you talking about? Katie, what's wrong?" He tentatively touched her. That was when he noticed the puddle around her feet. "Did that faucet spring another leak?" He moved to get past her and open the cabinet doors beneath the sink.

She laughed and placed a hand on his shoulder. "It's time, Matt."

He poked his head up from the cabinet. "Time for what?" But even as the words left his mouth, it dawned on him. "But, it's too early. It couldn't be. Could it?"

She only nodded in response.

"We have to go then, we have to get you to the hospital."

She smiled at him and shook her head. "I don't think..." she panted, holding one finger up to tell him to wait a moment, "...you should...drive. We'll never make it."

He laughed. "We're already halfway to the hospital this

time,'' he said, putting an arm around her and helping her walk through the kitchen and out to the garage.

"Call 9-1-1, Matt, just in case. You're about," she paused to pant, "to meet..." but she couldn't finish the sentence.

An hour later, in a cheery room on the third floor of the Lawford hospital, Matt cradled his son, and his daughter, in his arms. He counted their fingers, counted their toes, then looked at his wife and counted his blessings.

*　*　*　*　*

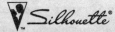

Silhouette Romance presents tales of
enchanted love and things beyond explanation
in the heartwarming series

Soulmates

Couples destined for each other are brought
together by the powerful magic of love....

Broken hearts are healed
WITH ONE TOUCH
by Karen Rose Smith (on sale January 2003)

Love comes full circle when
CUPID JONES GETS MARRIED
by DeAnna Talcott (on sale February 2003)

Soulmates
Some things are meant to be....

*Available at
your favorite retail outlet.*

Coming next month from

SILHOUETTE *Romance*®

Daycare DADS

**She can teach him how to
raise a child,
but what about love...?**

Introducing the amazing new series from

SUSAN MEIER

about single fathers needing to learn the
ABCs of TLC and the special women
up to the challenge.

BABY ON BOARD
January 2003

THE TYCOON'S DOUBLE TROUBLE
March 2003

THE NANNY SOLUTION
May 2003

You won't want to miss a single one!

Silhouette®
Where love comes alive™